For Keith and Brenda,
with best wishes,

Geoffrey Osborne

DEATH'S NO ANTIDOTE

One phone call is all it takes to shatter C.P.'s happiness and plunge him into a nightmare world of fear; a world of blackmail, kidnapping, torture . . . and death. He is forced to steal the DNA File, a secret formula which could be used by an unscrupulous Power to create a master race. But who are the blackmailers? Even C.P. doesn't know who he is supposed to be working for. When C.P. disappears from the Foreign Office with the secrets of the File, James Dingle and Glyn Jones, top agents of Britain's SS(O)S are already following a dangerous trail which crosses the paths of American, Russian and Chinese rivals. There are many surprises along the way as this tense drama (a sequel to " Checkmate for China ") moves relentlessly to its explosive climax.

DEATH'S
NO ANTIDOTE

by

GEOFFREY OSBORNE

ROBERT HALE & COMPANY
63 Old Brompton Road, London, S.W.7

First published in Great Britain 1971

ISBN 0 7091 2275 6

PRINTED IN GREAT BRITAIN BY
BRISTOL TYPESETTING CO. LTD.
BARTON MANOR - ST. PHILIP'S
BRISTOL

PROLOGUE

In a bachelor flat just off Albemarle Street and far enough away from Piccadilly to be insulated from its traffic noises, a tall, lean man hummed to himself. Not a pop song, because the man was a snob; but he considered Fingal's Cave to be a lively, happy piece of music. So he hummed it, because he was happy.

He had every reason to feel pleased with himself. At the age of thirty-four, just when he was beginning to despair of climbing higher up the Foreign Office ladder, he had been promoted; and he had been entrusted with highly confidential work. That meant there were no black marks against him. His nose was clean.

He had been seriously worried during the past year; but his fears obviously had been groundless. The new job, he knew, merited a positive vetting, but it had not prevented his appointment. The security people must have been satisfied. His nose was, without doubt, very clean.

There was another reason for his happiness. He was

in love; and in about an hour he would be meeting Susan, the girl who shared his somewhat high-brow cultural tastes and, occasionally, his bed. He had just returned from a visit to America on Foreign Office business, and so they hadn't seen each other for ten days.

" Ta ra ta-ta ta ta . . ."

His thick, rather unpleasant looking lips moved as he sang, bouncing apart like two pieces of rubber.

". . . ta-ra ra ra tum tum."

The telephone rang and he walked quickly across the room to snatch up the receiver. It was probably Susan.

" Julian Croome-Pugglesley speaking," he announced in his full, rich tone.

The voice that came back over the wire wasn't Susan's. His face grew pale as he listened.

" Who is that? Who are you?"

He listened again, and then slowly replaced the receiver which was wet with sweat from his trembling hand.

At that moment happiness died in him and the birth pains began of a new and terrible emotion. Fear.

* * *

Two hours later the Director of Britain's Special Security (Operations) Section picked up one of the five telephones on his desk, the black one which linked him to the outside world. He dialled a number.

"Dingle? Scramble please." He paused and then continued: "Remember Croome-Pugglesley? He's had a phone call . . . No, I don't know that yet. For the moment we'll assume it's the Chinese. They made a rendezvous . . . Yes, on Monday morning . . . No, he knows you, so Williams is taking care of that, but I want you in here by ten on Monday. Is that clear? And alert Jones, will you? I want you both here."

The Director replaced the receiver, and flicked up the intercom switch.

"Miss Peach, fetch me the files on Julian Croome-Pugglesley and on Counter-Intelligence (China)."

Next, he picked up the green telephone, the direct line to his control room.

"Duty Officer? Ah, Mr. Williams, you can use as many men as you think necessary on Monday—but ensure that none of them is known to Croome-Pugglesley. You'd better get the electronics department to help you in this. I don't want any mistakes. And arrange immediate surveillance. Discreetly, you understand. Someone else may already be tailing him.

CHAPTER ONE

THE DIRECTOR switched off the miniature tape recorder and leaned back in his swivel chair.

He peered from under bushy, white eyebrows which were pulled down so low that the skin around his deep-set brown eyes and on his high forehead wrinkled like corrugated paper. His mouth opened lop-sidedly to reveal dazzling white dentures. The Director was smiling.

Sitting facing him across the desk his two top agents, James Dingle and Glyn Jones, shifted uncomfortably. They thought he was scowling at them.

The Director nodded towards the tape recorder.

" The marvels of modern counter-intelligence. Almost every word, even though they were speaking in a crowded public restaurant." He shook his head in wonder. " I wish we'd had these electronic aids when I was an agent in the field."

" Have we identified Croome-Pugglesley's contact yet, sir ?" asked Dingle.

"Yes." The SS(O)S chief picked up a type-written report and began to read. "Fellow by the name of William Dawes. Bachelor. Age forty. Export salesman. Travels all over the world selling light aircraft."

Dingle and Jones glanced at each other.

"Plenty of opportunities for passing on information to agents overseas," observed Jones.

"Or for receiving instructions," said Dingle.

"Nothing known against him," the Director continued. "Successful at his job. Earns £10,000 a year. Lives in Kent, near New Romney. Modest enough house, but quite a lot of land attached. Part of it used as a grass air landing strip. A qualified pilot. Flies a company plane normally housed in a small hangar on aforementioned airstrip. Good service record. Was an infantry captain in Korea. Won the M.C."

He paused, put down the report and then added heavily: "Taken prisoner six months before the war ended."

"Ah!" said Dingle. "The link with China. Do you think he was brainwashed?"

The Director winced at the word. "Highly possible."

"How can we be sure that he is working for China?" asked Jones.

"We can't be sure, yet; but again, it's highly possible Don't forget, in the original phone call to Croome-Pugglesley, the late and unlamented Sir Roger Coyle was specifically mentioned."

" Dawes referred to Coyle as well when he kept the rendezvous with Croome-Pugglesley," said Dingle re-calling the tape-recorded conversation.

" Quite so. And apart from this department, only the Chinese know of C.P.'s involvement with Coyle.* Al-though," the Director added thoughtfully, " I'm willing to concede that the Russians might have unearthed the fact. They were closely connected with the affair."

" We'll assume it's the Chinese we're up against then," said Dingle. " So what's the next step?"

" I think you and Jones should call on C.P. and persuade him to co-operate with us."

" Poor old C.P. He won't know which way to turn," said Jones. " I wonder if he'll have a suitable quotation for this situation?" he added with a smile, remembering the Foreign Office man's habit of using Latin phrases.

" Dawes told C.P. that he wants details of the DNA file," said Dingle. " Do you know what he meant?"

The Director sighed.

" Yes, I do now. I made discreet inquiries through DI6—but I had to go direct to C** for the information. Wish I hadn't now. I seem to have stirred up a hornet's nest, and I've been summoned to a meeting of the Joint

*See Checkmate for China.

**" C " the traditional name for the knight who heads D16 (Defence Intelligence) formerly called M16. Also known as SIS (Secret Intelligence Service), and directed by Foreign Office and Prime Minister through " C ".

Intelligence Committee at the F.O. this afternoon.

"The DNA file belongs to the Americans. Reluctantly, it seems, they have allowed a copy to be brought over here for our own scientists to study and evaluate. Security is in the hands of DI6 . . . and, as we heard on the tape, the Foreign Office link man with Washington is Croome-Pugglesley."

"So C.P. has access?" asked Jones.

"He has."

"What exactly is the DNA file about, sir?" asked Dingle.

"C almost had a heart attack when he realised that I'd even heard of it," answered the Director. "Denied all knowledge of it at first, but he did give me a brief outline after I told him I knew about Croome-Pugglesley's connection with it.

"It seems that American biologists have isolated a key to heredity. DNA—or to give it its full name, deoxyribonucleic acid—is popularly known as the chemical of life. What the Americans have done is to isolate a single gene, a factor determining hereditary characteristics from DNA. Now they've taken it a step further."

Dingle looked up sharply. "Genetic engineering?"

"Exactly. They started to experiment with the idea of trying to obviate hereditary diseases or to change unwanted hereditary traits, such as weak eyesight, by injecting new genes.

" But now, it seems, the system could be used to purify any genes; those determining a person's size, muscle-power, IQ . . . the field is limitless."

The Director paused and leaned forward, hands flat on the desk and eyebrows raised to expose the two agents fully to the glare of his bright, intelligent eyes. When he spoke again his voice was lower, almost hushed.

" You realise the political implications? If this knowledge was used wrongly by a government or a dictator . . ."

He didn't complete the sentence. It was left for Dingle to say quietly : " They could produce a master-race. And China is trying to pinch the secret."

Glyn Jones was suitably impressed.

" Bloody 'ell Jim, boyo. Just imagine, millions of Chinese, all twelve feet tall, strong as horses and with their heads bulging with brains!"

CHAPTER TWO

CROOME-PUGGLESLEY'S nerves were raw. Over the past few days he'd had a permanent sick feeling in his stomach; he jumped at any unexpected sound, and he was becoming more bad-tempered than usual. Several times each night be woke up bathed in sweat.

Susan had noticed the change in him. She guessed something was wrong, and thought it was to do with his visit to America. She'd tried to comfort him; but all her attempts had failed. She tried again.

"Tell me what's wrong, Julian," she said. "I know something's troubling you. You've hardly spoken to me since you got back from America—and when you do speak you almost snap my head off." She tried to make her voice sound light. "Did you meet someone else while you were over there? Is that it?"

He looked at the almost icy beauty of her long, pale face, marred now by an anxious frown.

If only he could tell her, he thought. If only he could

tell anyone. But how could he? He was alone in his fear. It was a burden nobody could share.

"Of course I haven't met anyone else," he said. "I'm just a bit off-colour, that's all. It's nothing."

Her brown eyes were soft with concern.

"You should see your doctor."

"It's nothing, I tell you," he said angrily. "I'll have an early night and then I'll be all right."

"I'll make you a hot drink."

"No! I'll get it myself, later, when you've gone."

Her eyes widened in surprise.

"I thought . . . don't you want me to stay?"

He didn't answer. How could he explain that he had to be alone in the flat?

Susan got up from her chair, jabbed out her half-finished cigarette in the ash tray and tossed her head angrily, shaking her long black hair clear of her eyes which were blazing with fury.

"I see," she said through tight lips, moving quickly into the tiny hall, where she put on her coat without bothering to fasten it and picked up her overnight bag. She came back into the room for her handbag and turned again towards the door.

Croome-Pugglesley was on his feet.

"Susan!"

"Well?" Her tone was hostile.

"Be reasonable, Sue. All I said was . . ." Suddenly he felt his own temper rising, and he was shouting.

"For God's sake, what's the matter with you? You're behaving like a spoilt child . . ."

"Go to hell!"

She was running into the hall.

"Sue!"

But it was too late. The front door had slammed shut behind her.

*   *   *

Susan Pike didn't wait for the lift. She ran down the four flights of stairs to the street and walked quickly towards Green Park Underground station.

She felt angry and humiliated, and yet was aware of another underlying feeling akin to panic which threatened to rise to the surface.

She was seriously worried about Julian. Something had happened to him, she was sure. He seemed almost . . . frightened. She must find out what had changed him. But supposing, after this scene, he didn't want her back?

Her own fear welled up and threatened to choke her. No! It couldn't end now. It mustn't. There was a very special reason why.

She waited for the lights to halt the Piccadilly traffic so that she could cross. In the morning, she resolved, she would call him on the telephone and apologise, no matter how much it hurt her pride. The lights changed and she began to move again.

Even if she had not been so preoccupied, Susan would never have known she was being followed.

It was being done so expertly.

*   *   *

The anger and frustration ebbed from Croome-Pugglesley with the dying echoes of Susan's footsteps on the stairs. The sick fear began to take over again.

He tried to shrug off the feeling and went into the bedroom, switching on the light and pulling the curtains across before opening the drawer in the bedside table.

He took out a small package which had arrived in the morning mail, and sat on the bed to read again the note inside.

" As you will see from these prints, you haven't got the focus quite right. Practise some more—and use the enclosed stand. We feel that, when it comes to the real thing, your hands might shake too much to make a satisfactory job of it. Pass on film tomorrow, as before."

The note was unsigned.

He walked back into the sitting-room and opened the writing bureau. From an inside drawer, he took out the 8mm Minox B camera and fitted it into the stand.

He began to move more quickly, glancing at his watch to time himself. Opening his brief case, he took out a 200 watt bulb and swapped it with the one in the reading lamp.

A circular letter had arrived in the afternoon post.

He ripped it out of the envelope and smoothed it out on the desk. It wouldn't stay flat, so he used a paper weight and an ink stand to hold it down.

He adjusted the camera on its stand and peeped through the view finder, before switching on the lamp and arranging it so that the light fell just right.

A quick look at his watch. Thirty-five seconds. Completely absorbed now, he began to operate the camera. He took two shots of the circular, and then began to photograph every document within reach : insurance policy, passport, Premium Bonds. He worked steadily until the micro-film was used up.

Two minutes and twenty seconds. Damn. He'd have to be quicker . . .

He jerked round as though pulled by a string when the doorbell rang. His face paled and the left cheek began to twitch; but his limbs seemed incapable of movement.

The bell rang again.

He cursed himself for a fool. It was probably Susan; she'd come back to make it up.

He switched off the lamp and shut the camera inside the bureau. Then he crossed the hall to the front door, fixing his face in a smile as he went.

The smile slipped and his jaw sagged when he opened the door.

" Hello, C.P. boyo," said Glyn Jones cheerfully. " Remember us?"

" Er . . . er . . ."

" We just happened to be in the area," added Dingle, " so we thought we'd look you up. Aren't you going to ask us in?"

" Er . . . yes . . . of course."

Croome-Pugglesley led the way to the sitting-room and nodded towards the easy chairs.

" Sit down, won't you?" He tried to force a note of joviality into his voice. " Well, this is a pleasant surprise! What will you have to drink?"

" Nothing for us boyo." Jones was exaggerating his Welsh accent. " Not when we're on duty."

The reluctant host sat down abruptly on the settee.

" On duty?"

" Well, we don't drink when we're working, you see. I suppose we're like policemen, in a way."

" But you said . . . I thought this was a social call." Croome-Pugglesley tried to keep the tremor from his voice. " Oh, I see. Up to your old cloak and dagger tricks again eh? And you want me to help?"

" That's right."

" Well, what can I do for you?"

" Tell us all you know obout Dawes."

" Dawes?" Croome-Pugglesley looked puzzled.

" William Dawes," said Jones.

" Am I supposed to know him?"

Dingle, who had been gazing round the room, directed his gaze at the Foreign Office man.

" Do you deny that you met him in a restaurant on Monday: that he asked you to obtain a copy of the DNA file?"

" Oh my God!"

Croome-Pugglesley buried his face in his hands.

" I didn't even know his name. He never told me," he said miserably.

" And do you deny that he gave you a camera?" Dingle went on relentlessly. " You received a phone call last Saturday telling you where to meet him."

" You seem to know as much as I do. More. How did you get . . ."

Croome-Pugglesley jumped to his feet, suddenly angry.

" He was one of your men!" he shouted. " You're trying to trick me. This . . . this Dawes, or whatever his name is, is a SS(O)S man, isn't he? What are you up to?"

Jones shook his head pityingly.

" Bloody 'ell C.P., don't you even know who you're supposed to be working for?"

" I thought . . . I thought . . ."

" Well, what did you think?" snapped Dingle.

" I thought he was probably working for Russia. But he's one of your agents, isn't he?" There was a pleading note in his voice now. " What is this—a loyalty test thought up by Security?"

Dingle shook his head.

"No . . . and he's not one of our men. Our guess is that he's working for China."

"China!"

Croome-Pugglesley sat down again heavily.

"We're not drinking, C.P.," said Jones kindly, "but I think you could do with one."

The Welshman crossed to the sideboard, poured a generous measure of whisky into a glass and handed it to him.

"Thanks." The Foreign Office man gulped half of it down. "Are you going to arrest me?"

"Good heavens, no."

"What are you going to do then?"

"Nothing . . . if you help us."

Hope flashed into C.P.'s eyes. There might be a way out of this mess after all.

"What do you want me to do?"

"We want you to do exactly as Dawes asks. Give him a copy of the DNA file."

Croome-Pugglesley was feeling better now; more his old self. The drink had helped. He drew himself up to his full height and looked down at the two agents.

"Do you realise what you are asking? You are asking me—an official of Her Majesty's Foreign Service —to give classified information to a potential enemy," he said pompously.

"Come off it," said Jones. "You'd already agreed to do it, hadn't you?"

" I was just pretending. I was going to find out all I could and then inform Security at the F.O."

" And risk Dawes blabbing your part in the Coyle affair?" asked Dingle.

The man's new-found confidence sagged a little.

" You know about that, too?"

" We've always known about it. You've been under surveillance for the past year."

C.P. shook his head in disbelief. Then his assurance returned suddenly as a thought struck him. He even laughed.

" Thank you very much," he said. " Then you can all go to hell; you, your Director, Dawes, the Chinese . . . the lot of you. Don't you see what you've just done? You've let me off the hook! If my unfortunate connection with Coyle is already known to our people —and no action has been taken over it—then the Chinese having nothing left to blackmail me with. I'm . . ."

Dingle interrupted him.

" I said *we've* always known about you and Coyle . . . we being SS(O)S. It suited our purpose not to tell anyone else. The F.O. don't know."

C.P. subsided like a pricked balloon, back on to the settee.

" You bastards," he whispered. " It's blackmail. You're as bad as the Other Side."

" Are you going to co-operate?" asked Dingle.

22

"I haven't any choice, have I?" C.P.'s face was haggard.

"Good," said the SS(O)S man, heading for the door, followed by Jones. "Don't get up; we'll see ourselves out. Just carry on as you were. We'll be in touch."

"Wait," called Croome-Pugglesley. "If I help you, what happens to me at the end of it all?"

Dingle shrugged. "That's up to the Director. But he's after bigger fish than you, C.P., so I wouldn't worry too much."

"Ah yes, of course, the Director." C.P. smiled wryly at Jones. *"Anquila non capit muscas."*

Jones grinned back.

"Quite," he said.

"What was all that about?" Dingle asked when they were outside.

"An eagle doesn't catch flies," the Welshman translated for him.

CHAPTER THREE

THE BUZZ of conversation ceased abruptly when the Director stepped into the conference room at the Foreign Office. Every face—most of them hostile—turned towards him.

It was a full house, he noted. All the top brass were there. He sighed inwardly and advanced on the only vacant seat. Most of the other members of the Joint Intelligence Committee outranked him (his own official rank was Brigadier) and he could tell it was going to be a difficult meeting.

" Sorry I'm late gentlemen," he said, easing his over-weight frame into the protesting chair. " I thought you said three o'clock."

The Committee's Co-ordinator, a Deputy Under-secretary, who sat at the head of the table, looked at his watch and smiled.

" We did," he said. " And you're on the dot. The rest of us . . . ah . . . met a little earlier. We've been having a little . . . ah . . . discussion."

The Director scowled politely. I'll bet you have, he thought. I can almost feel the knives in my back.

"I think I'd better . . . ah . . . leave it to C to tell you what we've been talking about," the Co-ordinator added.

C, the Knight who headed D16, nodded agreement.

"Without going into details," he said, "I have been explaining that we have brought into this country a file—known as the DNA File—from America to be studied by our senior Ministry of Defence biologists.

"All the scientists who have access, of course, have been positively vetted. My own department is responsible for security relating to the file.

"I have asked our military friends here"—he glanced in turn at the Rear-Admiral representing the Directorate of Service Intelligence (DSI), the Air Vice-Marshal from the Directorate of Management and Support of Intelligence (DMSI) and their Director-General of Intelligence at the Ministry of Defence, a serving General in the Army—"and none of them even knew of the existence of the DNA file."

C inclined his head towards his fellow knight and opposite number at the Home Office, and continued: "None of our friends at D15 had heard of it, and nor had the Commander," he indicated the last man at the table, who headed Scotland Yard's Special Branch.

"So what I want to know is, how the hell did SS(O)S get on to it?" The words came out slowly and clearly

" I want to know how you know about the DNA File, and how you know that the Foreign Office link man with Washington is Mr. Julian Croome-Pugglesley.

" When I asked you this morning—after I had co-operated with you and given you certain information—you refused to answer. Now I am asking you again, officially, in the presence of the full JIC."

" And again I must refuse to answer," growled the Director.

C was white with anger.

" Do I have to remind you that D16 are responsible for security in this matter. I must know where the leak . . ."

The Deputy Undersecretary interrupted.

" May I ask on what grounds you refuse to answer, Director?"

" Because if I do, D16 and other departments might think it necessary to take action which could jeopardise certain inquiries being undertaken by my own department."

" In this country?" asked the Deputy Undersecretary.

" Yes."

" A bit off your beat, isn't it," said the D15 chief heatedly. " Counter-Intelligence and CE are my province."

" Exactly," chipped in C. " As I understand it, the main role of SS(O)S is to handle operations abroad which are . . ."

"Too bloody tricky for D16 to do efficiently," the Director finished nastily.

"I suppose you'll come running to us if there are any arrests to be made," said the Special Branch man, coming out to bat for the home team. "I think we should be consulted right from the start. I thought that was the function of the JIC, so that . . ."

"What do you mean by too tricky for D16," cut in C furiously, now that he had stopped choking. "You're just trying to lay down a smoke-screen to avoid answering my questions. As the person responsible for security on DNA, I must be told if you have information about a leak."

"And I repeat that to ensure the smooth running of my present operation, any information I have must be kept in a watertight compartment, namely SS(O)S."

The military contingent of the committee wriggled uncomfortably in their seats. Clearly the meeting was going to degenerate into another lengthy who-does-what? dispute. And, equally clearly, the military men thought the squabbling civilians should be lined up against a wall and shot, so that they, the Service men, could get on with the job.

C returned to the attack.

"But D16 . . ."

"Once employed Blake and Philby." The Director once more finished his sentence in a devastating manner.

While C was engaged in another choking fit, the Co-ordinator held up his hands.

" Gentlemen, gentlemen. We must be rational."

The Director looked at him quickly.

" May I see you for a few minutes, sir? Alone."

The D15 chief protested loudly, although secretly he was delighted at the D16 man's embarrassment.

" I don't see why he should see you alone Deputy Undersecretary." He emphasised the word deputy.

" I don't see why not," retorted the Director. " You all saw him without me before I arrived."

The Co-ordinator hesitated and then said quickly.

" Very well. In my office."

He rose and the Director followed him through the door which connected the Deputy Undersecretary's office with the conference room.

* * *

" You remember, about eighteen months ago, SS(O)S was given the task of ferreting out the Chinese espionage network in this country?" asked the Director.

" I do," replied the Co-ordinator. " It was felt that because you had done a lot of work in the Far East and had good contacts there, you might have the best chance of smashing the Chinese ring over here . . . by working backwards."

" Quite so. But we didn't have much luck until now. Remember the Coyle affair a year ago?"

" Of course."

" Well, Croome-Pugglesley was closely involved in that."

" I know. He was your liaison man with the F.O."

" He was also working for Coyle."

The Co-ordinator was startled.

" Good Lord! Why didn't you report this?"

" For two reasons: because he didn't realise what he was doing; and because it was highly probable that, later, the Chinese would try to blackmail him. When that happened, we might have a chance to penetrate their espionage set-up."

" And the Chinese have contacted him?"

" Yes. Last week. We've had him under constant surveillance. The Chinese already know about the DNA file; they must have found out from their agents in America. They've asked C.P. to get them a copy."

The Co-ordinator bit his lip.

" I think C has a right to know. D16 is responsible for Foreign Off . . ."

" I know that," interrupted the Director. " And C would have Croome-Pugglesley arrested and remove the danger at once. In his place I'd do the same."

" Well, then, can you reasonably withhold the information? After all, America is involved in this, and it . . ."

" I know, I know," the Director broke in again. " But it's worth taking a calculated risk. And it's not too big a risk because, I assure you, SS(O)S have a tight hold on the situation. And I honestly think it's our one big chance to lay the Chinese Dragon to rest in this country."

" Tell me everything, right from the start."

The Director told him all he knew, and, when he had finished, the Co-ordinator looked thoughtful and then asked, shrewdly:

" But how can you be sure that it *is* the Chinese who are after C.P.? You've no direct evidence."

" It's a reasonable assumption."

" Possibly, but it's not enough. I don't think we can keep the information you have away from the Joint Intelligence Committee. After all it exists to pool intelligence and co-operate."

" Give me a few days."

" I haven't the power to give such a ruling."

" The P.M. can, through you." The Director nodded at the red telephone on the Deputy Undersecretary's desk—a direct line to the Prime Minister. " Ring him."

The Co-ordinator hesitated.

" All right," he conceded grudgingly. " Go and wait with the others. But if I manage to get what you want, for heaven's sake try to make peace with C. Give him some sort of reassurance."

*   *   *

For the second time that afternoon, the Director's entry to the conference room was the cue for conversation to be cut short.

He walked back to his chair, lit a cigarette, and nodded affably to the others. The Service contingent inclined their heads politely in acknowledgement; the rest made no sign. Everyone sat in a stony silence broken only by C's fingers drumming irritably on the polished table.

At the end of half an hour the atmosphere was decidedly strained.

All heads turned at the click of the Co-ordinator's door handle.

"The jury's coming back," said the Director brightly.

The Commander, the D15 chief and C glared at him; the Service trio smiled.

The Deputy Undersecretary came in briskly and resumed his place at the head of the table.

"Sorry to have kept you waiting, gentlemen. I had to consult higher authority on this one."

He paused and looked at the SS(O)S man.

"You have a week, Director. After that . . ." he shrugged.

C's face was purple.

"You mean he can sit on this for a week? In that time . . ."

The Director cleared his throat and tried to make his voice sound conciliatory.

"I'm sorry I can't be more helpful to you C; but this is really a case of too many cooks spoiling the broth. The fewer people who know what my department is doing the better."

" If DNA is involved—and obviously it is—then it concerns my department," shouted the D16 head. " I have a right to know."

The Director drew in a deep breath. " I can assure you that there is no threat to your security," he lied easily. " And I can assure you that there has been no leak from your end. What I know was unearthed during an operation that SS(O)S has been engaged on for more than a year. If there has been a leak, it must have been at the American end."

C opened his mouth to reply, but the Director went on smoothly : " The P.M. has given me a week. I should like longer, but if my mission is no nearer completion at the end of that period, then I shall take you into my confidence."

" If that's the P.M.'s ruling . . .?" C looked at the Co-ordinator, who nodded . . . " then I have no choice," he added sourly. " But I don't like it."

" I quite understand your point of view," said the Director soothingly. " But I'm afraid I must ask you not to take any action which might ruin my operation. For instance, I don't want you to approach Mr. Croome-Pugglesley or alter your routine in any way."

" Ah ! So Croome-Pugglesley is involved?"

" I didn't say that. He . . . er . . . could help my operation; but I don't want him alarmed in any way. Now do I have your assurance C?"

There was a heavy silence, and then the D16 chief

said: "Very well. My department will leave Croome-Pugglesley alone for the time being. But I warn you that the security of the DNA file is my pigeon. I shall take any steps necessary to safeguard it."

"I think that's fair," said the Co-ordinator. "So if there's no other business . . .?" he glanced around the table . . . "then I think that concludes the meeting. Sorry to rush you, but I have another appointment with the P.M."

The Deputy Undersecretary watched the Intelligence chiefs file out of the room, and marvelled to himself that he should be privy to their secrets.

Obviously, he thought, I must have been positively vetted to hold this job. I wonder who did it? The Commander? Or some S.B. inspector who lives in a flat in Hammersmith?

His thoughts moved on to Croome-Pugglesley. Pity about young C.P. Came from a good family. Still he must be involved in this business; the Director was nobody's fool.

He sighed and made a mental note: must remember to cancel my dinner engagement with C.P.

CHAPTER FOUR

The judge's face was stern, unrelenting.

" The jury have, quite rightly, returned a verdict of guilty," he said.

Croome-Pugglesley turned to look at the jury. They stared back at him, indifferent, twelve pairs of dark, expressionless eyes.

They were all Chinese.

" You have brought disgrace on your country and on your family, a family with a great tradition of loyal service to the Crown," the judge continued.

C.P. looked more closely and saw that the face beneath the wig was that of his father.

" You have been found guilty of treachery of the worst kind. You are a traitor and deserve to be punished with the full severity of the law. You will be sent to prison for thirty years."

" No !"

C.P. cried out and tried to leap from the dock, but strong hands restrained him.

"Take him below," ordered the judge contempt-
uously.

C.P. struggled violently, but it was useless Blue-uni-
formed gaolers were holding him tightly, one on each
side. He saw that they had the faces of Dingle and
Jones.

"Let me go," he pleaded with them. "It wasn't my
fault."

But there was no mercy there.

And then another voice reached him.

"Julian! Julian! Let me help you."

It was Susan's voice. Sue, his only friend in the world.

A stab of light bruised his eyes and then he could see
her.

"Julian! What is it? What's the matter?"

She relaxed her grip slightly and he drew in a deep
breath. His pounding heart slowed down as he took in
the familiar surroundings. This was his own room. That
was his own clock, showing five past three. He was sitting up in his own bed.

"It's nothing," he said. "It was only a dream."

"You're sweating. Lie down and keep covered up or
you'll catch cold."

She forced him down and snuggled close to him.

"It must have been an awful dream. What was it
about?"

"Nothing. I can't remember. Did I say anything?"
he added anxiously.

" You were just shouting ' No ' and ' Let me go '."

Susan felt the tremors which ran through his body as he recalled the details of the nightmare.

Her gentle, soothing fingers stroked away the pain of fear. Her soft, warm kisses melted the icy needle of terror in his stomach and kindled a flame of desire.

Slowly, he became aware of her: of her slim legs wrapped about him; of her breasts pressed to him. He moved to face her, returning her caresses and kisses. The flame exploded into a volcano.

She felt his need, hard and urgent, drew him to her and clasped him tightly as they made love.

Afterwards, as he lay spent and exhausted, she leaned over his and spoke softly in his ear.

" What's troubling you, Julian? I know something's wrong. Let me help you."

He stiffened as awareness came flooding back.

" Please tell me, darling," she said when he didn't speak. " If something's worrying you, let me share it. I love you."

The sick dread was back in him now, numbing all other senses. The ticking of the alarm clock drew his eyes. Four o'clock. Thursday.

Today was the day. They'd ordered him to get the file today. In a few hours he was due to go on duty at the Foreign Office. And then . . .

" Julian! Please!"

Susan's voice penetrated his thoughts. He'd have to

tell her something. At least she might be an ally. She'd be on his side—if he didn't tell her the truth.

He stirred, and said: " It's work."

" Work? Your job at the F.O.?"

" Well . . ." he paused. " It's not exactly my job. I've been seconded to Intelligence . . . I'm working for Security."

" Security? You? You mean you're some sort of spy?"

" Agent. We call them agents." He added urgently: " But you mustn't tell anyone about this. It's highly secret and . . . and . . ." his voice hardened as he became carried away by his own fantasy . . . " I'm engaged on a dangerous mission."

Susan was impressed.

" No wonder you've been scared."

" Scared?" he said angrily. " I'm not scared. It's just the tension. I'm always like this before a mission."

" You mean you've done this sort of thing before?"

" Yes," he answered recklessly. " I'm a full-time British agent really. But you must never repeat what I've said. I trust you, Sue," he went on dramatically. " That's why I'm telling you. It's a lonely business . . . and I've got to confide in someone."

She snuggled up to him.

" You can trust me, darling. Is it really dangerous, this job?"

" Mission," he said. " Yes. I've got to get hold of something of vital importance to this country."

37

"When?"

"Today!"

"Today? Then by tonight it will be all over?"

"Yes," he said with feeling. "By tonight it will be all over."

CHAPTER FIVE

Miss Peach looked up and smiled when Dingle and Jones walked into her office. She liked and admired both of them; often, when they were working overseas, she worried about them.

Glyn Jones came in first, and she marvelled once more that his limp was barely perceptible. It was hard to believe that he had a false foot, the legacy of his first mission with Dingle.

The Welshman was forty-four, but looked ten years older. Pain and worry had ploughed deep furrows across his brow, but had failed to erase the crinkles of good humour which fanned out from the corners of his steady grey eyes.

Now that tired, lined face cracked into an answering grin.

"There's lovely you look! Give your dream boy a kiss," he said putting his arm around her shoulders and pecking her on the cheek. "Don't we look right for each other Jim boyo?"

"Peaches and Dream," said Dingle. "But take your hands off my bird. She's promised to go out with me, haven't you Peach?"

"I've told you before, I'm not a cradle-snatcher," replied Miss Peach, who was fat, jolly—and sixty-six. Past retirement age, she had been kept on by the SS(O)S chief who had once been heard to growl that his secretary was "the only indispensable person in the whole damned outfit."

"And as for you," she added to Jones, disengaging his arm, "you're not my dream boy—and I know all about you and that girl from the cipher office. Would you be unfaithful to her?"

"That's Glyn the Sin for you," commented Dingle. Jones looked thoughtful.

"Now why do you think our lovely Peach should reject two handsome, eligible bachelors like us, boyo? Is it possible that she loves another?"

Dingle pretended to consider the point.

"Perhaps she's in love with her boss," he said.

Miss Peach blushed and reached for the intercom, trying to hide her confusion.

"There's someone with him at the moment, but I'll tell the Director you're here," she said, pressing the switch.

"Yes?" The Director's voice made the loudspeaker vibrate.

"Mr. Dingle and Mr. Jones are here, sir."

"Send them straight in."

"Yes, sir."

She released the switch and looked at the two agents.

"You heard," she said.

"You know, Jim bach," said Jones as they moved towards the inner door, "I think you hit the nail right on the head."

* * *

The two men sitting opposite the Director stood and turned to face the SS(O)S agents as they came through the door.

Dingle was in the lead this time. Hard, lean and confident, his movements were those of an athlete in peak condition. His age could have been anything from thirty-eight to forty-five. Dark hair, flecked with grey, framed regular features of a face that was neither handsome nor ugly; an anonymous face.

"Mr. James Dingle, Mr. Glyn Jones, I'd like you to meet Mr. Gruber from NSA and Mr. Ritchie of the FBI," said the Director.

"Nick Gruber," said the first American, clasping Dingle's right hand and nothing that the British agent's index finger and the one next to it were missing.

Dingle had lost them on the same mission that had cost Jones his foot. Since then, he had learned to palm his automatic with the third finger, using his small finger to squeeze the trigger. Practice had made perfect. He had also taught himself to fire left-handed.

" I've heard a lot about you," the NSA agent added smiling. " Glad to meet you at last."

Gruber looked more like a professor than an Intelligence man. Slightly built, with thinning fair hair, he was three inches shorter than Dingle's five foot ten. But the Englishman guessed from his firm handshake that his slender frame concealed an immense wiry strength. Baby blue eyes blinked through gold-rimmed spectacles, studying Dingle so closely that he felt he was being mentally indexed.

" Pleased to meet you, too," said Dingle as the American relaxed his grip. " I don't know any of your chaps, probably because I've never been to Fort Meade. I know quite a few of the boys at Langley though."

Gruber's smile faded slightly.

" Sorry to hear you keep such bad company," he said. " You should steer clear of the pickle factory.* Some of the smell might stick."

He shifted his attention to Jones, and Dingle found his hand being crushed again, this time by the FBI agent.

*The headquarters of the Central Intelligence Agency is at Langley, Virginia. The members of the National Security Agency, whose HQ is at Fort Meade have dubbed the H-shaped CIA buildings as " the pickle factory ". The men of the CIA refer to the intellectuals with their sophisticated electronic spy gadgetry as " the boys across the street ". There is intense rivalry between the two organisations which has developed into a behind-the-scenes war. Some observers predict that the giant CIA will soon be virtually disbanded and engulfed by its rival, NSA.

"Jason Ritchie," the American introduced himself. "My friends call me Son."

Dingle grinned and extricated his hand.

"If you don't mind, Son, I'd like to hang on to the few fingers I've got left."

This man, he saw, was quite different to Gruber. Over six feet tall, his broad shoulders made him look shorter. Alert brown eyes were wide apart in a smooth, evenly-tanned face beneath close-cropped dark brown hair. The chin was round and strong, the mouth wide and humorous. The only thing that prevented him from being unbearably handsome was his nose. It looked as if it had been broken six times and remodelled by a drunken tree surgeon.

"You boyos are a bit off the beaten track, aren't you?" said Jones. "I thought you were home birds."

"Not at all," replied Gruber easily. "Both our out-fits are concerned with counter espionage. Sometimes our work takes us abroad—as in this case . . ." he paused and looked directly at Dingle . . . "And I think you'll agree Jim that the DNA file is very much an American CE matter."

Dingle raised his eyebrows politely.

"DNA file? What's that?"

The Director interrupted.

"I'm sorry gentlemen, but I must call our interview to a close. I have work to do with Mr. Dingle and Mr. Jones. I just thought I would introduce them to you before you left. You never know when your paths might cross in the . . . ah . . . line of business."

"Sure, sure. Don't let us hold you up, sir," said Gruber. "Thank you for sparing us your valuable time." He looked at Dingle and Jones and added: "I'm sure we'll be meeting again soon."

"It'll be a pleasure," said Dingle.

When they had gone, the two British agents sat in the seats vacated by the Americans.

"Who steered them in this direction?" asked Dingle.

"I'm not sure," answered the Director. "It could have been C. On the other hand, they say they are paying courtesy calls on the heads of all our security sections to let us know they are operating over here. It seems they don't want to tread on our toes."

"There's polite," said Jones. "A funny partnership though, isn't it sir, NSA and FBI?"

"There again, they were careful to explain that while the FBI were making a routine check for security leaks in the DNA file, some of NSA's electronic equipment picked up a coded reference to it on a top security line in China. So the two organisations are co-operating.

"Gruber made sure he mentioned the DNA file to me a few times—without saying what it was, of course. Obviously he wanted to see my reaction."

The Director looked at Dingle. "I'm glad you didn't give anything away when he tried it on you James. I thought I'd better let you meet them. They might get under your feet while you're working on this job, so it's just as well for you to know who they are.

" Now then," he went on brusquely, " what about Croome-Pugglesley? Have you heard anything from him?"

" He has been in touch, sir," replied Dingle. " This morning. He says he has had instructions to photograph the contents of the file today. They told him how he is to hand the film over tonight."

" Can he do it?"

" He thinks so."

" Have you given him any instructions?"

" I've just told him to do exactly what the Other Side tell him to."

The Director leaned forward, resting his paunch on the desk.

" Keep me posted of all developments. Glyn, you must keep James covered at all times—and the pair of you will have to make sure those blasted Americans don't get in your way. There must be no mistake on this one. If there is a mistake, it'll be the last any of us will make."

He nodded his head in dismissal. " As you go out, tell Miss Peach I want her."

The two agents walked through the secretary's office to the outer door and into the corridor.

Then Jones stuck his head back round the door and said : " Oh, Peach, you're in luck. Your dream has come true. The boss told me to tell you he wants you."

The Welshman leered and emphasised the word " wants ".

He closed the door just in time. He heard the heavy metal stapler crash against the other side.

CHAPTER SIX

C TAPPED the stem of his pipe irritably between his teeth and stared at the document on his desk.

In ascending order of importance, official documents are classified as restricted, confidential, secret and top secret. NATO have an even higher classification called NATO cosmic. Beyond this, documents become personal, to be opened only by the person to whom it is addressed.

The one on C's desk was personal. He picked it up and read it for the fourth time, slowly and carefully. It said :

Additional data dispatched updating DNA file. Ensure tightest security. Information suggests leakage Chinawise. Investigating this end. NSA and FBI agents Gruber and Ritchie will make contact to assist your end. Co-operation vital.

It was signed by the head of the US Joint Intelligence Committee State Department.

C put down the flimsy document and leaned back in his chair, closing his eyes to think.

This note which had reached him the day before,

was the first hint he'd had that China might be involved. The two American agents had called on him only half an hour ago—but they had been unable, or unwililng, to add anything more concrete than that a message mentioning DNA had been intercepted in China.

China! He remembered that SS(O)S had, in the past, carried out operations against China. Perhaps that was how the Director had got on to it. He took comfort from the thought.

He recalled the Director's statement at the JIC meeting: "If there's been any leak, it's probably at the American end."

The sudden alarm in the Washington camp lent weight to this. But why was the Director so anxious that Julian Croome-Pugglesley should not be alerted?

Possibly, he thought, the SS(O)S chief expected C.P. to be approached—or even kidnapped with the DNA file. In which case the Director's men would be watching C.P. very closely. But suppose—the D16 head shuddered at the thought—suppose something went wrong and C.P. vanished with the file.

The safety of the file in this country was solely the concern of D16; yet the presence of the NSA and FBI agents suggested that his American opposite numbers doubted the efficiency of his department. C strongly resented this.

He opened his eyes and saw again the final two words of the message: *Co-operation vital.*

48

Damn the Director, damn the Americans, damn them all. He'd co-operate all right. He'd keep the DNA file sewn up so tightly for the next four days that nobody could get at it. At the end of that time the Director of SS(O)S would be forced to come clean to the JIC.

Until then, he'd co-operate to the best of his ability. That was why he'd hinted to the American agents, without being specific, that it might pay them to contact SS(O)S.

Until then, he'd concentrate on one thing : keeping the secrets of the DNA file secure.

He reached for the phone.

*   *   *

In a much smaller room on the next floor of the Foreign Office the internal phone on Croome-Pugglesley's desk buzzed insistently. Without shifting his gaze from the papers in front of him, C.P. picked up the receiver.

" Yes?"

" Have you received an addition to the DNA file?" asked C.

" Yes sir. It's in front of me now. An addition and some minor alterations. I've just sent for the file. It's being taken down to the research labs in Wiltshire this afternoon so that the boffins can study it, so I'll have to get it done before . . ."

"Cancel that," said C quickly. "Delay the file's departure for four days. Got that?"

"Yes sir. But what . . .?"

"I want to check security down there and I want a further screening on the scientists who will have access. By the way, do you ever take the file out of the building to work on at home?"

"Good lord, no sir. It's top secret material and I . . ."

"Well just make sure you don't. When you've finished bringing it up to date it must not leave the strong room until it goes down to Wiltshire four days from now. Is that clear?"

"Yes sir."

"And another thing," C's voice became almost a whisper over the wire, "watch out for yourself when you're outside the office."

The knot in C.P.'s stomach tightened.

"What do you mean sir?"

"Someone might approach you about the file."

"Approach . . .?"

"I can't be specific. But if the Other Side have got wind of the file, they might try to . . . ah . . . bribe you or even . . ." the voice dropped even lower . . . "resort to physical violence. Do you understand?"

C.P. tried to swallow. His Adam's apple seemed to be stuck to the dry walls of his throat.

"Are you there?"

" Yes, sir." The words came out hoarsely. " You mean they might . . .?"

" Abduct you, kidnap you." C's voice was back to full strength now, tetchy and impatient. " Now do you understand man?"

C.P. reached out a shaking hand for his cup and swallowed cold drags of tea to ease his parched throat.

" For heaven's sake, man! Are you there? Can you hear me?"

" Yes sir. But what makes you think there might have been a . . . a . . .?"

" Leak? Because I've just had a visit from two American agents. They hinted at something of the sort."

For the first time during the conversation, C.P. raised his eyes from the papers on his desk to look at the two men sitting opposite. He said into the phone : " With me now sir."

" Eh? What? Ah, I see! You can't say much. I understand now." C's tone was less sharp. " Well, remember what I said and watch out for yourself."

The line went dead. C.P. replaced the receiver, slowly, to give himself time to think and to get his voice working properly again.

He looked at Gruber and Ritchie.

" I'm sorry, gentlemen, but I . . ."

A knock on the door gave him a further respite. Two security guards came in, one of them carrying the DNA file.

" Put it on the desk," said C.P., " and then wait out-side. I'll only be about ten minutes, and then I want you to take it back to the strong room."

" Sir?" said the man with the file, glancing doubt-fully at the two Americans.

" These gentlemen are leaving now," said C.P. smiling at his visitors and shrugging apologetically. He was back in control of himself now. " I'm afraid you're not allowed to remain alone with me in my office when I have a top secret file in my possession . . . and, as you see, I am rather busy."

" Sure, sure, we won't hold you up any longer Mr. Croome-Pugglesley," said Gruber, rising to his feet.

" There's just one more thing, though," said Ritchie. " Do you know of an outfit called SS(O)S?"

C.P. felt as if a net was being tightened about him.

" Er . . . no . . . yes."

His control was slipping again and he was having more trouble with his voice.

" Have you had any contact with them, or perhaps worked with them?" asked Gruber.

" No . . . that is, yes. In the past. Why?"

" Oh, we just wondered," replied Gruber easily. " We're just off to their chief—the Director I think they call him."

He held out his hand.

" Well, thanks for all your help Mr. Croome-Pugglesley."

Alone at last, C.P. leaned back in his chair and breathed deeply, trying to relax his stomach muscles which had tensed into a hard band. Afterwards he used his handkerchief to mop his brow and dry the palms of his hands.

He stared dully at the fat file lying on his desk. Then with a start he remembered the two security guards. He walked quickly across the room and opened the door.

" Have those Americans gone?"

" Yes sir."

" Good. I'm going to lock my door while I'm working, but I shan't be long. Don't go away, and don't let anyone disturb me. The file must be returned immediately."

" Right sir."

He closed the door and turned the key. Back at his desk he opened the file and began to work quickly, making the few minor corrections and slotting in the added material. It took only five minutes.

The routine work calmed him, and a faint smile quirked at the corners of his mouth as he saw humour in the situation.

So this was how simple it was for spies to steal secrets —although he was probably the first to do it with a couple of Foreign Office security men guarding the door for him.

" *Cavendo tutus* "* he said softly, opening his brief
*Safe through taking care (Lat).

case to take out the camera, the stand—and a 200 watt bulb, which he swopped with the issue 60 watt bulb in his desk lamp. The discarded bulb began to roll across the top of the desk, so he picked it up and placed it carefully in a drawer.

Swiftly, the way he had practised at home, he fitted up the camera on its stand and switched on the lamp, arranging it so that the white splash of light fell exactly right—on the first page of the open file.

There were sixty-nine pages. The only sound in the room was the rustle of the sheets being turned over, punctuated by the click of the camera. Once he paused, after using the thirty-six exposures on the 8mm micro-film, to slip in a new cartridge.

He worked on methodically, unhurried, absorbed in the task, making no mistakes. It took exactly eleven minutes.

A knock on the door startled him while he was dis-mantling the camera. His heart raced and suddenly he was bathed in sweat. His knees were weak as he moved across the room.

"Yes?" he called out, his mouth close to the thick wooden panel of the door.

"Are you nearly finished sir? There's a young lady waiting here, wants to bring you a cup of tea."

Relief flooded through him.

"Oh. Yes. Just a minute."

He almost ran to the desk, snatched up his brief case and stuffed the camera and stand inside. He snicked the catches home and put the case in the empty bottom drawer of a steel filing cabinet, which he locked.

Then, just as he was about to open the door, he saw the harsh glare of the light on the desk. He switched off the lamp and moved it back to its usual position on the desk.

" Sorry to have kept you waiting," he said, unlocking the door to admit the two security guards. " The file's on the desk. You can take it back now."

" Your tea will be stone cold," scolded a young secretary following the two men into the room. " Shall I fetch another cup?"

" No, this will do fine, thank you."

" I've got a pile of memos in my room for you that need answering," the girl added. " Shall I bring them in now?"

" Yes, all right. Might as well get them out of the way," replied C.P.

For the rest of the day he was too busy to think about the brief case locked away in the filing cabinet.

CHAPTER SEVEN

SIX-THIRTY. The dank November air was a cold flannel on his face. Shopfront illuminations blazed in colourful defiance, lighting up the damp pavements; but already the street lamps were eerie orange spheres, floating independently in a hazy ceiling. It would be foggy soon.

C.P. noticed none of this. He was aware of only one thing: the brief case under his arm—and the films that nestled inside like twin time bombs. They could be, he thought, his passport to freedom. Freedom from fear. Or they could be his death warrant.

He glanced apprehensively over his shoulder, wishing he'd been able to find a taxi, remembering C's warning.

But why should the Other Side attack him now. They were going to get what they wanted; or they thought they were. He would just have to trust Dingle and Jones. Soon he would be finished with this nightmare. In less than an hour, this business should be over and done with.

He recalled the instructions that had been dropped

through his letterbox two nights ago. He was to go
straight home and place the films in the biscuit barrel
in his kitchen cabinet. At seven o'clock precisely, he was
to go out, leaving the front door of the flat ajar, taking
with him the camera and stand. These he was to dispose
of before walking to Piccadilly to buy a packet of cigarettes. By the time he got back to the flat the films would
be gone.

When he had told Dingle about the instructions, the
British agent had ordered him to follow them exactly. He
wondered what Dingle planned to do.

C.P. stopped to buy an *Evening Standard* at a news
stand.

" Goin' ter be a real pea-souper guv," observed the
newspaper seller.

" Eh? Oh, yes," replied C.P., seeing for the first time
the fog which was now beginning to clamp down.
When he reached Albemarle Street, it was really thick.

As he turned into the entrance of the apartment block,
he whirled around in fear at the sound of running footsteps behind him.

" Julian! Is that you? I thought I'd missed you in
this fog."

" For God's sake, Susan! You gave me a fright."
The words were spoken sharply, but there was a tremor
in his voice. He looked around nervously, seeing nothing
in the gloom, and began to whisper urgently. " You
can't come here now. You must go away, quickly."

She came nearer and held his arm.

"What's the matter?" She was whispering, too, sensing his unease. "Is it the job? You said it would be over tonight . . ."

"Yes it's the job," he hissed. "Get away from here now. It could be dangerous for you. I'll come to your place when I'm finished."

"Can I help you . . .?"

He pushed her away roughly.

"Will you do as I tell you!"

"All right . . ." already her form was melting into the murky night . . . "but don't forget."

C.P. didn't bother to reply. He ran up the steps into the tiny lobby of the apartment block, pressed the button for the lift and glanced at his watch. It was already ten minutes to seven. Impatiently, he stabbed at the button again and then realised that the lift wasn't working.

Smothering a curse, he made for the stairs, running up them two at a time. His chest was heaving when he closed the door of his flat behind him. He crossed the small hall to the lounge, switched on the light—and started violently, biting back a shrill cry of terror.

"You'll have to watch those nerves of yours C.P.," said Dingle, pocketing the automatic that had been pointing at the Foreign Office man's stomach. "I thought it was you puffing and panting away out there. You need more exercise."

58

" The lift's not . . . how did you get . . . what the hell are you doing in my flat?"

Reaction was setting in now; anger was taking over from fear.

" I'm waiting for your friends."

" Oh! How long have you been here?"

" All afternoon. I didn't want them to see me coming in."

" What are you going to do?"

" That's my business; you attend to yours. It's nearly seven."

C.P. moved to the table and unzipped his brief case. Taking out the films, he hurried with them to the kitchen and dropped them into the biscuit barrel.

Back in the lounge, still wearing his gloves, he spread out the newspaper he had bought on the way home. Then he took the camera and stand from the brief case and began to wipe them clean.

" My God, Dingle, I'll be glad when this is over. And you'd better keep your end of the bargain."

" What bargain?"

" You promised that if I helped . . ."

" I promised you nothing," Dingle interrupted. " I said it would be up to the Director to decide what to do about you. And I've no idea what he'll decide."

" You bastard! You . . ."

C.P. stiffened suddenly; his face flushed and hot sweat bathed his body.

" What's wrong?"

" Nothing. It's nothing," muttered C.P., bending to wrap the photographic equipment in the newspaper.

But there was something wrong. He'd made a mistake; but it would be all right. No one would notice. He could put it right tomorrow.

" It's seven o'clock," said the SS(O)S agent.

" I'm ready now."

" Switch all the lights out after you. And don't forget to leave the front door on the latch."

*   *   *

Glyn Jones shivered and stamped his feet to keep warm. He grinned to himself. You fool, boyo, it's no good stamping your right foot because it's not there. Still, it's queer you'd look stamping just one foot. Brrrr . . . trust that Dingle to pick the nice warm inside job. I'll bet he's sitting back in a . . .

The Welshman tensed into alertness, then stepped back out of sight. A man appeared under the light at the entrance to the apartment block, ran down the steps and vanished into the fog, leaving only the fading, hollow ring of footsteps to prove that he had ever been there.

Jones pulled out a pocket radio and spoke into it softly.

" Are you there, Willie?"

" Yes." Williams's voice came back in a metallic whisper.

60

" C.P. has just left."

" Good. Is Jim still in there?"

" Yes . . . wait a minute, there's a car coming."

Williams, in the driving seat of a battered looking van fifty yards up the street, turned to the three men squeezed in the back.

" Hear that, did you?"

" Yes. It's about time something happened," answered one of them. " I'm perished."

" Fat chance we've got of following anyone in this lot," said another.

Williams chewed nervously at his lip. The problem of tailing a car in the fog without being spotted had been worrying him for some time.

" We mustn't lose them," he said. " We've got to see where they go. It's the top men we want, not the messenger boys."

The radio crackled into life.

" It's stopped in front of the entrance," came Jones's voice.

" Which way are they facing?"

" Towards you."

" I'll turn round and park on the other side of the road, a bit further up. As they come past, I'll fall in behind. Let me know when they move."

" Right."

" How many men are there?"

" Don't know. No one's got out yet."

" I'll wait to hear from you."

Jones heard the muffled sound of the van turning round. He watched the car, wondering why nobody got out.

* * *

C.P. walked slowly down Albemarle Street, almost feeling his way, until he found what he wanted. A narrow passage leading to the back of a restaurant.

There was no glimmer of light here, and he shuffled along, touching the wall with the back of his gloved hand.

After what seemed an eternity, he found the door which led to a yard at the back of the restaurant. He opened it and heard the clatter of dishes coming from the kitchen. A ghostly glow came from the windows, but it didn't help.

He found the dustbin by falling over it. There was no lid. Wrinkling his nose distastefully, he lifted some of the garbage and slipped the camera and stand, still wrapped in the newspaper, underneath. Tomorrow, they would be collected by the refuse lorry and disposed of. If, by chance, they were ever found by a scavenger, they would never be traced to him.

C.P. groped his way back to the street and stood undecided. His instructions were to waste more time by walking to Piccadilly to buy cigarettes. But he didn't feel inclined to walk in this fog.

He turned back towards home. He could always wait outside until he thought the coast was clear.

*   *   *

Dingle listened at the partly open door to the sound of C.P.'s footsteps going down the stairs. Soon a heavy silence fell over the building.

Flicking on a pencil torch, he moved softly back into the lounge and looked through the window. The fog was too thick to see the road below. But he heard the sound of a car drawing up.

He walked swiftly, then, to the kitchen. By the light of the torch, propped on a table, he opened the cabinet and lifted the lid of the biscuit barrel.

There couldn't be much time. He would have to work fast and then hide in the bedroom.

A familiar prickling sensation at the back of his neck warned him. But this time it was too late.

He whirled round, dodging a blow from the barrel of the pistol held by the first man. He even managed to land a solid blow on the jaw of the second man. But he couldn't avoid the cosh wielded expertly by the third.

Dingle crashed to the floor, dazed, wondering dully how his assailants could possibly have got up from the car so quickly.

And then, in a flash of understanding, he realised that they hadn't been in the car. They had probably

63

been waiting for some time on the floor above until C.P. left. The car was probably there to take them away.

The cosh descended again, viciously.

The three men stood around Dingle's prostrate form.

"Who is he?" asked the second man, rubbing his jaw. He spoke with difficulty.

The man with the pistol, obviously the leader of the group, answered him.

"You haven't been doing your homework, have you? Look at his right hand."

The man who had done the damage, the one with the cosh, said: "He's got two fingers missing. So?"

"Turn him over and get a good look at his face," said the leader impatiently, switching on the light.

Using his foot, the cosh expert rolled Dingle roughly on to his back.

"Now do you recognise him? His photograph and description are in the files at HQ."

Understanding dawned in the pain-filled eyes of the man with the injured jaw.

"Dingle!" he exclaimed. "It's Dingle the SS(O)S . . ."

"Brilliant!" interrupted the leader. "You should have recognised him immediately. But the pair of you would have passed him by in the street without a second glance. And yet he's listed in the file of dangerous enemies—which you are supposed to have studied and memorised thoroughly."

He paused and added slowly: "The question is . . . what is he doing here? Did Croome-Pugglesley contact him, or have SS(O)S been watching . . .?"

"Obviously he was after the film," the cosh man intervened brightly.

"Your powers of deduction amaze me," said the leader sarcastically. He lifted the lid off the biscuit barrel and took out the two exposed films. "But he was too late. I saw what he was doing."

"I think we'd better assume that Croome-Pugglesley didn't know Dingle was here . . . he must have been hiding somewhere in the flat. SS(O)S must have been watching that Foreign Office twit all along . . . so they must have known, or guessed, what he was up to."

Cosh looked startled.

"You mean they know about us?"

"They may not know who we are. Probably the plan was to retrieve these films," answered the leader, slipping them into his pocket, "and then either pick us up—or follow us—when we came to collect them."

"You mean Dingle's not alone?"

"I should consider it highly unlikely. There are probably others outside."

"Let's get out of here," said the man with the injured jaw. "We've got what we came for."

"No, wait!" The leader looked down at Dingle. "Is he dead?"

Cosh knelt down and felt the British agent's pulse.

" No."

" Shall I finish him off, boss?" asked Jaw, eagerly.

" No," replied the leader quickly, making a decision. " We'll take him with us."

" We'll what!"

" He might come in handy as a hostage if we have any trouble getting out of here—and I think the Colonel would like to meet him again. Quickly now! Take him between you, I'll go down in front of you and make sure the car's ready."

*   *   *

Glyn Jones sensed that he was no longer alone. He could feel, rather than see, someone moving quite close to him; moving stealthily.

Part of the darkness just to his left seemed blacker, more tangible than the rest; a shape began to emerge from its protective, foggy cocoon to take on a more solid form. There was the sound of a shoe scraping on the gritty road surface.

Jones edged away. The shape followed him, forcing him to move even further back. Then it stopped.

The Welshman smothered an oath. He couldn't see the entrance so clearly now; but the light above the door, filtering weakly through the murk, was just strong enough for him to se a man run down the steps. The engine of the car coughed into life.

It was at this point that Jones began to feel things

were going wrong. By this time Dingle, still up in the flat, should have contacted him over the radio. But the tiny loudspeaker plugged into his ear remained silent.

He watched the car anxiously, uncertain what to do. He should warn Williams in the van—but if he spoke on the radio, he would betray himself to the other, unknown watcher.

The man who had come out of the building was standing on the pavement, holding open the rear door of the car.

Two more figures appeared, hurrying down the steps. They were dragging a limp form between them which they bundled into the car before climbing in themselves. The door slammed shut.

The first man was getting in the front of the car when Jones moved.

" Get ready, Willie. Something's wrong !" he shouted into the radio, no longer caring who heard him. Then he was running hard towards the car.

He never reached it.

Flame spurted from the man's hand, and Jones crashed face-down in the gutter as the sound of the shot cracked out. Then the man was in the car, which was already moving forward.

Headlights flicked on, reflecting back uselessly from the wall of fog. The front nearside wheel missed the Welshman's head by inches as the driver swung round in a U-turn, steering blindly.

The car lurched on to the opposite pavement, the lights momentarily picking out the terrified face of Croome-Pugglesley as he dodged clear of its path.

Bouncing back on to the road, the driver dowsed the headlights and switched on the yellow foglamp, which gave him a view of the kerb for a distance of about twenty feet.

The rear lights vanished into the blackness—in the opposite direction from the van in which Williams and his crew were waiting.

With the sound of the engine still screaming in his ears, C.P. ran across the road to Jones. He turned the Welshman over and tore off his glove to feel for a pulse. He lifted Jones's head—and withdrew his hand quickly with a sharp cry of horror.

He could not see what it was that felt so wet and sticky; but he knew it must be blood.

Dimly he was aware of somebody crouching beside him.

" Who is he?"

C.P. started at the sound of the voice.

" His name is Jones. A British agent," he answered dully. " What are you doing here, Sue? I told you to . . ."

" I had to come back to see if you were all right," the girl said quickly. " What are you going to do about . . .?" she broke off at the sound of running footsteps and the slamming of a vehicle door. " There's someone coming!"

68

C.P. stiffened. " They mustn't find me with . . . with him." He was unable to keep the tremor out of his voice.

" Quickly! Come to my place," said Susan. " I'll hide you."

As they hurried away into the fog, a silent witness slipped out of the cover of a nearby doorway.

He walked quickly away in the same direction as C.P. and the girl.

CHAPTER EIGHT

JAMES DINGLE couldn't pinpoint the pain, couldn't separate one hurt from another. His twisted body was being jolted against something hard, increasing the agony.

He felt sick; and above the buzzing noise in his throbbing head was another sound . . . a car engine. He must be on the floor of a car . . .

Cautiously, he tried to turn in the cramped space to ease his aching limbs. His outstretched hand touched something which quickly moved away.

His hair was grabbed roughly from above and his head jerked back. Something cold, hard and round was pressed against his mouth. He couldn't see it, but Dingle knew it was the barrel of a revolver.

"Take it easy and don't move Jimmy, or I'll riddle yer," said a harsh voice. The man began to laugh coarsely. "Get it Alf? Jimmy Riddle."

Alf didn't join in the laughter.

"That's how I'd like to see the bastard . . . riddled,"

he said viciously. His words were slurred, as though he had difficulty in speaking.

"Cut it out you two."

This voice was authoritative, educated. It sounded vaguely familiar and came from the front of the car; but Dingle couldn't see its owner.

"You're even tougher than we'd been led to believe, Mr. Dingle," the smooth voice continued conversationally. "I thought you'd be out for hours. We still have some way to go—and it'll take even longer in this fog —so I'm afraid we'll have to put you to sleep again."

"I'll do it, boss," said Alf.

"All right . . . no, not that way! Give him a shot with this."

"It'll be easier it I just . . ."

"I said give him a shot. The Colonel will want him in one piece."

Dingle heard the voices, but the words held no meaning. The pain, the threats were irrelevant, swamped in a new sensation.

Fear.

He could feel the fear rising from his stomach, climbing up his throat, with the bile, into a soundless scream.

He raised trembling hands to his face, but his wrists were grasped strongly.

"Hold him Dave," said Alf.

The revolver was removed from his mouth. Fresh hands held his wrists in a vice-like grip. He felt his left sleeve being pushed up roughly, stiffened instinctively as the needle was driven home.

But it wasn't that which made him cry out. The injection was as irrelevant as the rest. Fear had been overtaken by something else.

Panic.

He began to struggle violently. Strong hands and, sometimes, feet held him down, pinning him to the floor. Soon the strength born of panic left him, drained from his body by the greater, insidious strength of the drug.

"Help me!" His voice was a tortured sob. "For God's sake, help me. I'm blind!"

And then, mercifully, James Dingle slept.

* * *

Julian Croome-Pugglesley didn't like Susan's friends. It was an instinctive feeling. They had left the room now, to make coffee.

"Why couldn't we have just stayed in your flat?" His voice was petulant.

"I told you. The people who are after you might know that I'm your . . . your fiancée. They might go looking for you at my place."

"Well, who are these people? And why did you have to leave me alone with them for so long."

"Harry and Marjorie Brett and friends of mine. I had to go out to phone another . . ."

Harry Brett opened the door for his wife who was carrying a tray of coffee and biscuits.

They were an oddly matched couple. The man, about forty, had long, soft brown hair, delicate pink flesh and a plump little body. His wife was taller, flat chested, with a long hard face. Her hair was shorter than her husband's, and going grey. She wore no make-up. She was wearing trousers.

" Well this is nice," said Harry Brett. C.P. noticed that he spoke with a slight lisp. " I'm glad you thought of us, Sue dear. Fancy getting stranded in the fog."

" We were so close to your place, I thought . . ."

" Of course you did quite right to come to us," said Mrs. Brett. " We'll be only to pleased to put you up until the morning. You can't go out again on a night like this."

She didn't sound too pleased, C.P. thought. Her voice was deep, husky.

" It's extremely kind of you," he said.

" Where did you say you abandoned the car?" asked Mr. Brett.

" About a mile away," said Sue quickly.

C.P. flinched again at the lie. Suppose their hosts found out in the morning that they didn't have a car. After leaving Sue's flat they'd taken a train from Liverpool Street to Edmonton, and then jumped aboard a 649 bus that had crawled the rest of the way to Ponders End.

All the time the Bretts were talking, he had the feeling that they were listening for something; waiting for something. They didn't seem surprised when the front doorbell rang.

Mrs. Brett jumped up to answer it. She came back into the room with a tall, big-boned man who she introduced as Mr. Finn.

C.P. stood up to shake hands, but Mr. Finn kept his own hands in his pockets.

" Please sit down Mr. Pugglesley."

" Croome-Pugglesley."

" Yes, but I shall call you Pugglesley. I do so hate these snobbish British double-barrelled names. No, not there," as C.P. was about to sink back, flabbergasted, into his armchair. " Over there." Finn indicated, with a nod of his massive head, a hard, straight-backed dining chair.

" I don't understand," said C.P. stiffly. He looked at his hosts and at Sue.

The three stared back at him without expression. It was then that he felt a sudden lurch of fear in his belly.

" You don't understand?" Finn chuckled. " You will Mr. Pugglesley, you will. I won't bother to beat about the bush. I want some information from you, and I want it quickly."

" Who are you?"

" I am . . . we all are . . . officers of the KGB. I won't bother to give you our real names." Finn's voice was suddenly charged with menace, his grey, soft-steel eyes hardened into tungsten. " Now sit down."

Somehow, C.P.'s shaking legs carried him to the chair.

" I shan't tell you anything." He looked in mute appeal at Sue, who gazed coldly back at him.

Harry Brett tittered.

" Shall I fetch the whip dear?"

C.P. saw the sudden gleam in Mrs. Brett's eyes, but it was Finn who answered.

" I don't think that will be necessary. I think Mr. Pugglesley will see the reason of a much more subtle argument."

*   *   *

Jason Ritchie poked his head through the driver's window.

" About time you got here."

" I've been as quick as I could in this goddamned Limey fog," answered Gruber. " Which is the house?"

The FBI man pointed across the road.

" That one."

" They still in there, Son?"

" Yep."

" So what now?" the man from NSA asked.

" So now you can watch. I'll take the car round the corner and have a nap. We'll take it in turns. I'll relieve you in two hours . . . unless anything happens before then."

Nick Gruber climbed out of the car.

" It's going to be a long, cold night," he grumbled.

CHAPTER NINE

WILLIAMS SHUFFLED uncomfortably from one foot to the other. He hadn't been invited to sit down.

"So between you, you've balled the whole thing up," the Director growled.

"It was the fog, sir. We couldn't see a thing. I heard Glyn Jones telling us something had gone wrong . . . then the sound of a shot, followed by a car moving off. But it took us some time to realise the car wasn't coming our way."

"And Jones? What did the nursing home say?"

"He'll live sir. A flesh wound in the neck; and apparently he cracked his head on the kerb when he fell. He was still unconscious when I left."

"Did you have any trouble getting him away?"

"Not really. A few people turned up—with a policeman somebody had called. I got him to ring Special Branch. They cleared us, and I got the boys to take Glyn to the nursing home in the van."

The Director nodded. "And Dingle?"

" No sign of him sir. I searched the flat before I went to the nursing home."

" Hmmm. Let's hope that at least he's doing something to save the situation." The Director had a lot of faith in Dingle. He added : " And what about Croome-Pugglesley?"

" No sign of him either sir."

" All right, get back to the nursing home and hold Jones's hand. I want a full report from him the minute he can speak. Understand?"

" Yes sir."

Williams escaped thankfully.

* * *

" He's regained consciousness then?" said Williams, relieved.

" Yes," said the doctor. " But he's sleeping now. You can't talk to him."

" I've got to. You'll have to wake him up doctor."

" I'll do nothing of the kind. He's under sedation. He'll have to sleep it off."

" Did he say anything when he came round?"

" Nothing that made any sense."

" I'll sit with him until he wakes up, then," said Williams.

* * *

It was six o'clock when Williams jerked awake at the sound of Jones's voice.

"Hello, Willie bach. What are you doing here?"

The Welshman tried to sit up, and sank back with a groan.

"Bloody 'ell, where were we last night, Willie? My head feels like a . . ." he broke off and awareness flooded into his eyes. "Hey! They shot me!" A note of panic crept in. "Is it bad, Willie? Am I dying?"

"A graze on the neck and a bump on the nut, that's all."

"Oh." Jones sounded vaguely disappointed.

"Thank God you can remember what happened, anyway. The Director . . ."

He was interrupted by the doctor entering the room.

"Ah! You're awake. I've just had your boss on the phone. Wanted to know how you are. He sounded most concerned about you. I told him you'd be all right after a few days rest."

Jones was sitting up again, with more success this time.

"What did he say to that?"

"He said you could have a few days rest."

Jones looked at the doctor in wonder.

"Dew! Did he say that? Did he actually say that?"

"Yes. He said, 'I'll give him a few days rest'."

Jones pushed the bedclothes back, swung his legs to the floor, stood up—and sat down again abruptly.

79

" I'd better get back to HQ and make my report."

He tried again, and this time succeeded in remaining upright.

" You're not going anywhere," said the doctor. " Get back to bed."

" Make your report to me," said Williams. " I'll relay it to the Director. That's why I'm here."

The Welshman's head was throbbing; his neck was stiff, and each movement made him dizzy with pain.

" Have you got a car with you Willie? You can give me a lift."

" You'll get a lift in a hearse if you don't do as you're told," said the doctor angrily. " I can't allow you to leave."

" I'm discharging myself. Get the car round to the front door, Willie. You can give me some pills for this headache, can't you doc?"

The doctor shrugged, accepting defeat.

" All right; but you'll have those wounds dressed again before you go."

* * *

" He's on the phone . . . but I'd better break in and tell him you're here," said Miss Peach, reaching for the intercom switch.

She paused, looking again at the bulky dressing on the Welshman's neck.

"Are you sure you're all right?"

"Sure. It was only a bullet." Jones the wounded hero. He lifted his shoulders in a nonchalent shrug. The movement sent a searing stab of pain through him, transforming what was intended to be a brave smile into an agonised grimace.

Miss Peach's finger travelled on and flicked the switch.

"What is it? You know I'm busy." The Director's voice was even more tetchy than usual.

"Mr. Jones is here sir."

"Here? Send him straight in."

The Director waved Jones to a chair, an angry flush on his face as he listened to the voice at the other end of the telephone.

"I'm asking you again, officially, to take no action yet," said the big man. "Leave it to us. Yes . . . yes . . . I'll take full responsibility."

He slammed the phone down and glared at Jones.

"You've cocked this one up, haven't you?"

The Welshman wriggled uncomfortably, sending another wave of pain through his body from his injured neck.

"That was C on the line. He says Croome-Pugglesley didn't turn up at the F.O. today . . . so he had the man's office searched. They found the regular bulb from his desk lamp inside a drawer, and a powerful one in the lamp. Now C's convinced that C.P. photographed the

DNA File yesterday. I can't think why the idiot didn't take the bulb away with the camera last night."

" Perhaps he didn't have time sir."

" And why hasn't he gone to work this morning? You and Dingle were supposed to be taking care of all this —and Dingle still hasn't reported in . . ."

One of the telephones buzzed urgently and the Director snatched it up.

" Yes? She hasn't . . . not there either? You've been inside . . .? Nothing. All right, come back in."

The Director replaced the phone and pressed the intercom.

" Is Mr. Williams in the building?"

" Yes sir."

" Tell him I want him in here immediately."

The SS(O)S chief leaned back in his chair.

" That girl friend of C.P.'s hasn't gone to work this morning either," he said. " There's no one in her flat, and her bed hasn't been slept in.

" Now there are three questions I want the answers to: Where is C.P.? Where is the girl? And where the hell is Dingle?

" I've had Williams's report, for what it's worth, on last night's fiasco. Now I'll have yours."

The tablets the doctor had given Jones were beginning to take effect. The pounding in his head had almost stopped; the pain from the bullet wound was blunted. Until now, his recollection of the previous night's events had been hazy; but memory was flooding back. The Director's last question tore away the remaining shreds of the curtain that had shadowed his mind.

He closed his eyes and conjured up a foggy picture. Two dim figures running down steps . . . a third, limp shape between them . . . a car . . . a blinding pain . . . and then . . . nothing

" I think they've got Jim Dingle sir," he said quietly.

The Director sat bolt upright.

" What!"

Jones told him everything he could remember.

" Did you recognise any of these men?"

" No sir. I told you, I was too far away. There was someone else moving near me in the fog and I was forced to shift . . ."

" Mr. Williams is here sir." Miss Peach's voice, harsh and metallic over the intercom.

" Send him in."

The Director waved Jones to silence and rifled through a file on his desk. He found the page he wanted as Williams entered the room.

" This Susan Pike girl," he said without preamble. " It says here she's been a secretary with the BBC for four years."

" Yes sir," answered Williams.

" Her parents died just over four years ago in a car crash in . . ." the Director paused . . . " in Russia. She flew out there for the funeral; couldn't afford to have the bodies flown home. Then she came back, sold up the family home in Taunton and moved to London. What were her parents doing in Russia?"

"Holiday, sir. First trip abroad. We checked the booking with a Taunton travel agent. They were on a package tour. The accident happened in a hire car just outside Moscow. Head-on collision with a lorry. The Russian chauffeur was killed, too."

"Yes, yes, that's all in this report," said the Director. "Plus the fact that the girl has an uncle who emigrated to Australia fifteen years ago. No other living relatives. Met Croome-Pugglesley a year ago at a party . . ."

The SS(O)S chief broke off and looked at Williams.

"How well was this girl screened?"

Williams licked dry lips.

"Normal vetting sir."

"Really?" The Director's eyebrows shot up. "I should have thought that she would have rated a positive with this Russian link."

"Only a tenuous link, sir," said Williams bravely.

"Tenuous?" The big man's voice was deceptively mild. "Not as tenuous as your future prospects as a section head in this organisation Mr. Williams. The girl has disappeared. So has C.P. They were last seen together by Jones shortly before last night's farce. She was waiting outside C.P.'s place for him to come home. When he arrived he sent her away. Your job is to find both of them. And I want quick results."

For the second time that morning, Williams made a thankful escape from his chief's office.

"And your job," the Director added to Jones, "is to find James. Any ideas?"

"Only one lead I can see sir. I'd like a free hand to follow it up."

The Welshman leaned forward and began to speak.

*   *   *

"C? You can take any action you like on Croome-Pugglesley now. I don't think it will interfere with my own operation any longer."

A choking sound came over the wire.

"You don't think . . . Now look here . . . It's long past time you told me what you're up to . . ."

"My time isn't up yet," the Director said. "On the P.M.'s authority. Remember?"

"Yes, I remember all right," answered the head of D16 bitterly. "But I think the circumstances have changed."

"In what respect?"

"You know damn well, blast you! I'm virtually certain that Croome-Pugglesley has photographed the DNA File. Now he's gone missing. On top of all that I've just received a SB report that one of your men was shot last night—outside Croome-Pugglesley's flat. I suppose you'll say that's coincidence."

" Quite. I wouldn't worry about that C. Incidentally, if your people do find C.P., perhaps you'd let me know. Just for interest's sake, you understand?"

" I'm warning you," said C, " I'm going to request a meeting with the P.M. and put all the fresh facts before him. I'm sure he'll reverse his decision." He added grimly : " So you'd better hold yourself ready for an emergency meeting of the JIC."

" Just give me another twenty-four hours," said the Director. " That's all I need. And I assure you that everything is under control . . ."

He stopped speaking. C had already rung off.

Everything under control, he thought as he replaced the telephone. And I don't even know for sure yet who we're up against. To think that I was telling Williams that *his* future was bleak.

He picked up the red telephone.

" The P.M.'s in Scotland, opening a power station," said the Deputy Undersecretary. " I can get him for you if it's urgent. He'll be back at No. 10 early tomorrow morning."

" No, it doesn't matter," said the Director.

That was one bit of luck, anyway. It was doubtful if C would get the P.M. to change his mind before to-morrow.

CHAPTER TEN

CROOME-PUGGLESLEY was proving unexpectedly difficult.

" I'm not a traitor," he repeated woodenly.

He was slumped uncomfortably on the hard chair and he looked exhausted, drained of all emotion.

" I realise you have no wish to betray your country," said Mr. Finn. " But I'm afraid you are already a traitor by default. It began when you failed to reveal your liaison with Sir Roger Coyle. You helped him when he was actively working for China . . ."

C.P. stiffened. " How do you know about that?"

" You forget, the KGB were co-operating with your own SS(O)S in that affair. We deduced, accurately as it turned out, exactly where Coyle was getting his information."

" It seems everyone knows about it," said C.P. tiredly. " Everyone except the Foreign Office."

" Quite. I suspect the SS(O)S kept you under observation in the hope that you'd lead them to someone else. We, on the other hand, planted the lovely Susan Pike on you, in the event that we might be able . . ." he broke off abruptly, and then added : " I presume it's the Chinese who have been putting the pressure on you recently? Blackmail?"

C.P. didn't answer.

Finn sighed. " You know you are finished in this country? Your people will try you for treason. Surely you don't want to rot in an English prison for twenty or even thirty years? Is it the Chinese?"

C.P. remained silent.

" What did they want? What have you been doing for them?"

Still no reply.

" Whatever it was," Finn went on, " it seems that SS(O)S knew about it, otherwise what was Jones doing outside your flat? And look what happened to him. Do you want to end up the same way?"

C.P. flinched, remembering the blood he'd washed from his hand. Jones's blood. He was sure Jones was dead. Dingle, too, perhaps. He'd seen his unconscious body being flung into the car . . . the car that seconds later had mounted the pavement in the fog and almost ran him down. They would not be able to help him now.

C.P. felt no pity for Dingle or Jones. He hated them for the impossible position they had put him in; he felt pity only for himself.

" Why don't you see reason?" Finn's voice droned on.

" Your career, everything, is ruined here. What do you think the security services and the police will do when you don't report for work in the morning? They're bound to link you with Jones. His body will have been found outside your flat. You might even be charged with murder as well as treason."

C.P. felt faint. He leaned forward, pushing his head between his knees.

" Be sensible. Tell us what we want to know. We'll look after you, take you to Russia where you can live a life of . . ."

" Leave me alone," said C.P. miserably. " Just go away and leave me alone."

" Very well." Finn's voice hardened. " If you won't co-operate voluntarily, we'll have to make you. Harry, I think it's time you fetched that whip of yours."

Brett snickered and waddled out of the room. Marjorie Brett's pointed tongue darted out and flicked at her dry lips; her eyes gleamed in eager anticipation.

Susan Pike spoke for the first time since Finn had revealed that she was a KGB agent.

" There's no need to hurt him!"

She moved quickly across the room and placed a protective arm around C.P.'s shoulders.

He arched his neck, straining his head back against her yielding breasts so that he could look up into her face. There was bewilderment in his eyes.

" What are you trying to do to me?"

" I'm trying to help you, darling. I love you, Julian.
We're going to be married, remember?"

" I know there's no need to hurt him," Finn's voice
broke in harshly, " but his attitude makes it necessary.
Now get away from him."

" Do as they say, Julian. Please, for my sake." Sue
cradled his head. " For both our sakes. If you come back
with us to Russia we can be married. We can have an
apartment in the best part of Moscow, holidays on the
Black Sea . . . they'll give you a well-paid job. We'll live
in luxury, darling. Please . . ."

" I said get away from him," Finn cut in again.

The girl released C.P. and drew apart.

" But it's true, isn't it?" she asked. " What I said?"

" Of course it's true," answered Finn, " but the man's
too much of a fool to realise . . . ah, there you are
Harry. Come into the kitchen with me . . . and you,
Marjorie. We'll collect a few more items of equipment,
and I'll explain what I'm going to do." He tossed a
revolver across to Susan. " Watch him."

When the others had left the room, C.P. whispered
hoarsely.

" Sue! Do you mean it? Do you still love me . . .
want to marry me?"

" Of course. Darling, don't let them hurt you. Help
them! We could be happy together . . . in Russia."

" You help me, Sue. Now, while they're out of the
room. We can get out through the window."

He half rose from the chair, but sank back when Susan brought up the gun, pointing the barrel straight at his chest.

" I daren't Julian . . . I . . ." she paused, and he could see the indecision on her face.

" We could be happy together here . . . in England," he said eagerly.

" It wouldn't work. If we got out of here, what would we escape to? You couldn't escape trial darling, not now. They'd take me, too. We'd both end up in prison . . ."

" Take a chance. If we went straight to the authorities now, tonight, and told them all . . ."

The girl laughed flatly, cutting off the rest of the sentence.

" And if it worked, if we remained free, do you think my people would let it rest at that? They'd send someone for me, later. I'd be taken back home and . . . and punished. Besides," her voice was tired, toneless, " I have relatives in Russia. I must think of them."

" Please, Sue . . ."

But it was too late. The others were coming back into the room.

" Strip him, and then tie his feet to the chair," ordered Finn, taking the gun back from Susan. " Leave his hands free."

C.P. didn't bother to resist. He knew it would be use-less. Soon he was naked, sitting awkwardly on the hard chair again, his ankles bound tightly and painfully to the chair legs.

"And now his girl friend."

C.P. gasped. "Why her? She's on your side."

Susan didn't speak. But her eyes gazed into Croome-Pugglesley's begging him to do what Finn wanted.

"Because, my dear Pugglesley, she is in love with you. You are in love with her. You are going to feel pain. She is going to feel the same pain. You will know exactly what she is going through. Sooner or later you will tell me what I want to know."

Rivulets of sweat began to course down C.P.'s face. Soon Sue was standing before him, as naked and defenceless as he. The thought of that beautiful body, the body that he knew so well, being scarred and broken made him shudder. But he didn't speak. Perhaps Finn was only bluffing . . .

Another hard chair was brought in and placed back-to-back with his. Susan's feet were lashed to its legs.

"We're going to begin quite gently." Finn's voice was matter-of-fact. "As you see, our make-shift equipment is quite simple."

He waved a hand towards the table, and C.P. looked at a collection of sharp kitchen knives, a candle, matches, needles . . . and a whip.

"Do you know what it feels like to have needles pushed up under your finger nails?" The tone was still conversational. "Hold his arms tightly, with the hands facing out towards me . . . that's right."

C.P. gave a sharp cry and jerked convulsively as the pain shot up his right forefinger, reaching for every nerve in his body.

"There now, that wasn't so bad was it. But still, there are nine more nails left to work on. You can have a short rest now, while we do the same for your girl friend."

The sweat was streaming down C.P.'s face now. He couldn't see Susan, behind him, but he heard her sharp intake of breath, and then the air expelled in a long shuddering sob. She didn't make as much noise as he had.

*　　*　　*

By turning his head he could see the clock on the mantelpiece. Had he been enduring this agony for only ten minutes?

Sue's high-pitched scream jumped the gap between them to join the silent, tormented screams of his own body, uniting them in pain. Poor Sue . . . and then the dreaded figure of Finn was standing in front of him again.

"There really is no need for all this you know. You're being unnecessarily stubborn. Are you ready to speak yet?"

C.P. shook his head dumbly.

Finn sighed. "All right. But I warn you, you're not going to like this one. Tie his hands behind the chair, Harry, and hold his head very firmly, slightly to one side. That's right . . . now light the candle Marjorie."

Mrs. Brett was breathing rapidly with excitement as she brought the lighted candle across to Finn.

C.P. tried to pull his head away, but it was held in a vice-like grip. He whimpered softly when Finn poured some of the hot candle grease into his ear, and again when the woman buried the live head of a match into the soft wax.

He felt the scorching heat of the candle when it lit the other end of the match. As the flame began to travel down the matchstick, the heat increased. His back arched in agony and he let out a long, low moan.

The burning in his ear became unbearable, his body writhed uncontrollably—and then there was an explosion in his head as the live end of the match flared inside the candlewax. His body sagged limply, held to the chair by its bonds. C.P. had fainted.

*　　*　　*

"There we are old chap. Have a drink, brandy . . . it's good stuff; and a cigarette."

Finn's tone was still light, friendly. C.P. gulped greedily at the golden liquid in the glass held to his lips by the big man. He sucked hungrily at the cigarette.

His ear was stinging; it felt like a huge throbbing balloon on the side of his head.

"That's better," Finn went on. "We had to wait for you to come round before we dealt with Susan . . ."

"No!" C.P. meant to shout the word, but his voice was a croak.

"And then, of course, we'll operate on your other ear."

"No!" said C.P. again. His voice was stronger now.

"No?" Finn's eyebrows raised.

"Damn you! What do you want to know?"

Finn smiled. "That's better. Marjorie, go and get hot water, soap, disinfectant and some ointment. You can be dressing his wounds while we talk."

He turned back to C.P.

"Who are you working for? The Chinese?"

"I don't know. Dingle and Jones thought so."

"You don't know?"

"I dealt only with one man. He was English."

"Who was he?"

"He didn't tell me his name. Dingle said he was called William Laws . . . no . . . Dawes. William Dawes."

"Describe him."

C.P. gave a detailed description, wincing every now and then when Mrs. Brett hit a tender spot. She was working swiftly, efficiently soothing away his aches and pains, cooing over him like a mother over a favourite son. He had pleased her intensely by allowing her to witness his pain. She enjoyed pain. She looked at the whip on the table. Perhaps later, when everyone had gone, Harry would . . .

"What did Dawes want?" Finn's voice went on remorselessly.

"The DNA File. I had to photograph it."

"The DNA . . . what's that?"

C.P. explained. The words poured out in a torrent.

* * *

"That'll do," said Finn. "Take him up to bed and make him comfortable. I'll see him again in the morning. Keep a sharp eye on him though."

The Bretts helped C.P. to his feet. He saw Susan, her head slumped forward on her chest, still tied to her chair.

"My God! What have you done to her?"

"She'll be all right," said Finn. "Harry and Marjorie will see to her when they've got you to bed."

Sue lifted her head and smiled bravely at C.P.

"I'm all right darling," she said. "Everything will be OK now. You'll see, when we're in Russia . . ."

"I should hardly think your friends will want to take me with them now," said C.P.

Finn sighed patiently. "Why not? There's no future for you here now. You've betrayed your country over

and over again. Believe me, I didn't want to hurt you
. . . either of you. But it was necessary. You must see
that. Now up to bed with you. You'll feel better in the
morning—and you'll see that your only hope is with us."

He waited until C.P. was upstairs with the Bretts,
then turned to Susan and untied her bonds.

" Well my dear, we didn't hurt you, did you?"

" Not a bit," replied Sue, smiling.

" I must say your screams were most convincing."

" I'm glad it's over anyway," said the girl. " At least
I don't have to pretend any more."

" Pretend?"

" That I'm in love with him. I can't bear the man. I
hate it every time he touches me. Those thick lips . . .
ugh . . . he's repulsive." She shuddered.

" I'm afraid you'll have to put up with it for a little
longer. At least until we get home."

The girl's eyes widened. " You're not taking him
back to Russia with us? He's told all he knows."

" Maybe, maybe not. In any event, he might be useful to us for a while. We don't want any trouble from him
anyway. I've got to go out now. I'll have to trace this
man Dawes . . . and I've got to find out what happened
to the films that Pugglesley took."

He walked towards the door and then paused.

" Meanwhile," he added, " you can join him in bed.
Convince him that he'll be better off in Russia. That's
an order."

CHAPTER ELEVEN

A VAGUE, unidentified noise roused Dingle from his deep, drugged sleep. Instinctively, he stayed perfectly still. A conditioned reflex warned him of danger, but his mind refused to specify it.

He sensed that he was not alone; somehow he knew it was important not to advertise the fact that he was awake. He listened carefully, and fancied he caught the sound of breathing, slow and regular, like someone sleeping.

Dingle tried to think; tried to remember where he was. He was lying on his back on something soft. A bed? But where? It certainly wasn't his own bed. His arms were stretched out, above his head. They felt stiff.

Cautiously, he moved his arms—but not far. Something was restricting them. They were tied to the bed-posts. He tried his legs and found that he could move them, but not separately. They were bound together at the ankles.

Slowly, he opened his eyes. But there was nothing

but blackness. He was aware of a pressure round his head. Bandages . . .?

Memory flooded back like a shock-wave.

He recalled the events of the previous night . . . the fight in C.P.'s flat . . . coming round in the car . . . and his last despairing thought before succumbing to the drug.

He was blind.

He fought to control the panic that was rising again in him; and then stiffened at the sound of a door being opened.

" Morning Dave. Any trouble? Did you get any sleep?"

Dingle recognised the voice from the nightmare car journey.

Dave Chance, alias Cosh, yawned. " I dozed a bit. He's still out cold. Hasn't even moved. How's your jaw?"

" Still hurts. I thought the bastard had broken it."

Dave laughed. " He had a worse fright. He thought he was blind."

Alf Gunney, alias Jaw, joined in the laughter.

" We needn't have bothered with the blindfold. He was in no condition to see where we were taking him anyway."

Relief flowed through Dingle. He wasn't blind! He wasn't blind after all. He suppressed an almost hysterical desire to echo his captors' laughter.

" You'd better go to the kitchen and get some break-fast while it's still hot," said Gunney. " Turner's just cooked it. I'll watch the sleeping beauty for you while you're away. I've had mine."

" Thanks. Is the boss about?"

" Yes. He's busy on the phone. I think he's going up to . . . oh . . . here he is."

The door opened and Dingle heard another voice. A voice with a familiar ring to it. He'd half recognised it in the car last night. He tried to remember where he'd heard it before. There had been something different about the pitch before, as if he'd been listening to it on the radio or . . . that was it! A tape recorder! He'd heard it in the Director's office. The voice of the man who had blackmailed C.P. into working for him. William Dawes, the pilot.

" Everything all right in here, Chance?" asked Dawes.

" Yes boss," said Dave.

" Had your breakfast?"

" I've just come to relieve him," said Alf.

" Good. Before you go Chance, while you're both here, I'll give you your instructions. I'm going up to London soon to fetch the Colonel. While I'm there I'll be making arrangements to fly to Athens tonight on a sales deal . . ."

Gunney chuckled. " Via Albania, boss?"

" Exactly. The Colonel thinks we should get away as

quickly as possible, now that we have the films. We'll be taking friend Dingle with us."

"To China?" That was Chance's voice.

"Yes. He's wanted there for crimes against the People's Republic. The Colonel is looking forward to meeting him; apparently he has an old score to settle."

Dawes paused, and then went on. "While I'm in London it will be up to you to guard Dingle very carefully. You'll be in charge Gunney."

"Yes boss."

"Don't take any chances. At least two of you must be with him at all times. Keep his wrists tied to the bedposts and keep his legs tied. If you give him any food, unfasten one hand only. If he wants to go to the lavatory, all three of you will go with him. Is that clear?"

"Yes. Turner isn't driving you up to London then?"

"No. He's putting my own number plates back on the car at the moment, then he'll be coming in here. You might as well get your breakfast now, Chance. I'll keep Gunney company until Turner gets here."

"Right! I'm starving!"

Dingle heard Chance's footsteps cross the room. The door opened and closed, then Dawes said:

"It's time Dingle was coming round. Let's get the blindfold off him and see if we can wake him up."

Dingle waited until the blindfold had been torn away before he opened his eyes.

" I'm already awake Mr. . . ." he bit off the rest of the sentence. No sense in letting Dawes know that he already knew his name; that he was blown. " I'm afraid you have the advantage. I don't know your name," he finished.

The pilot gave a mock bow. " Dawes. William Dawes," he said. " Have you heard everything I've been saying?"

Dingle nodded.

" Then you will have gathered that tonight I shall be flying you to Albania, and from there you will be taken to China?"

Again Dingle nodded. " You're not going to China yourself then?"

" No, just you and the Colonel. I'm an aircraft sales-man, you see, and I'm flying to Athens on a perfectly legitimate business trip. I'll make a refuelling stop at Rome—and then I'll touch down briefly in Albania to drop you and the Colonel."

" Ah, I see. Er . . . who is this Colonel you keep talk-ing about?"

" Colonel Fu Chang-sui of the People's Liberation Army."

Dingle couldn't hide his start of surprise.

" Colonel Fu? He's here?"

He wondered what the deputy head of Red China's Military Intelligence was doing in Britain.

CHAPTER TWELVE

C.P. SNATCHED his arm away from Susan and sat up in bed.

"You might have knocked," he said irritably. "We might have been . . ."

"What, straight after breakfast?" said Finn. "Anyway, you weren't . . . were you?"

"That's beside the point."

"Oh, shut up," said Finn, sitting heavily on the side of the bed, "and take a look at these." He tossed a folder to C.P.

The Foreign Office man opened the folder and about a dozen photographs tumbled out. He picked them up carefully, wincing slightly. His fingertips were still sore from Finn's attentions of the previous night.

"Who are these men?" he asked.

"Recognise any of them?"

C.P. studied the portraits, shaking his head as he discarded the first eight. But the ninth riveted his attention.

" That's him . . . Dawes . . . the man who contacted me."

" You're sure?"

" Quite sure."

Finn took the photograph, smiling with satisfaction.

" I thought that might be our bird." He turned it over and read the notes on the back. " One of our agents in Peking found out that he was working for China. That was way back in the days when our relations with Mao were more amiable. We even used to co-operate then . . . up to a point. We keep our own file on known Chinese agents. Luckily for us Dawes is included."

Susan sat up and took the photograph. C.P. noticed again that her nails were coloured deeply with red varnish, and he felt a renewed rush of tenderness for the girl. Obviously she was hiding the scars of Finn's torture. Female vanity being what it was, she didn't want the marks to show. Oddly, she seemed to bear Finn no malice. It had all been done for the good of the cause; to bring him to heel.

" Do we know where this Dawes lives?" she asked.

Finn nodded. " In Kent, near the coast. He has a private air-strip there."

" An air-strip?"

" Yes. He's a pilot."

Susan gave a start. " Do you think . . .?"

" That he's flown off with the prize? No, I don't think so. Not yet. The fog's only just clearing, for one thing. And he'll probably have arrangements to make. He couldn't have been a hundred per cent certain that Mr. Pugglesley would leave the film for him last night. If he's going to fly the film out, my guess is that he'll try tonight. I hope so, anyway. We'll pop down to Romney this afternoon and take a look around."

Finn stood up. " Meanwhile I have some arrangements of my own to make."

Before he left the room he added : " And if you don't want to be disturbed in future, you'd better lock the door."

*   *   *

Ten-thirty. The fog had gone, but the sky was a uniform grey except for a few breaks in the cloud over the Channel.

Glyn Jones gently moved his head and shoulders, trying to ease the stiffness in his neck. He shivered, not because he was cold, but because this desolate corner of Kent always depressed him, even in the summer. As a winter resort it rated very low in his personal popularity chart.

He'd made fast time down to Romney Marsh. It was nearly eight o'clock and still dark when he'd left SS(O)S headquarters, heading south-east on the A20 to join the M20 at Wrotham.

He ignored the speed limit and took the Lotus up to

a ton on the motorway, gritting his teeth against the pain from his wound. There was only one thought in his mind : to find Dingle. And after last night's disaster he had only one lead : Dawes. If that lead frizzled out, if Dawes had vanished as effectively as everyone else . . . Jones had shut that possibility out of his thoughts.

Just past Bearsted he rejoined the A20, took the Ashford by-pass and, at Hythe, turned right along the coast road. He found the place between Dymchurch and St. Mary's Bay, just off the New Romney road. He drove on for about a mile, parked the car off the road and walked back.

Now he stared thoughtfully at the roof of the house which was all he could see above the low trees and fence which surrounded the extensive property.

He walked past the entrance to the drive, climbed a gate into a field and approached from the rear. The boundary fence was only six feet high and presented no problem, even with his injury.

Jones dropped lightly into the bushes on the other side and moved forward. The house was out of sight at this point.

The bushes ended abruptly and gave way to a broad tarmac apron, and Jones found himself looking at the rear of a hangar. There was nobody in sight.

Swiftly he crossed the apron, ran alongside the hangar and looked into the gaping front doors. He was still alone.

The SS(O)S agent slipped inside and glanced at the gleaming twin-engined executive jet which was parked there. It was a best-seller of the company Dawes worked for—and Jones imagined that one of his sales gimmicks would be to give potential buyers demonstration flights.

He turned and looked out through the doorway. From here he had a much better idea of the layout of the property which ran from north-west to south-east in a broad oblong.

The runway ran straight ahead from the hangar to the south-east boundary, which bordered the coast road. On his left he could see a large garden which gave way to a small orchard in the south-east corner. Set into the garden, on his left and slightly in front of him was a garage. Beyond that was Dawes's home. It wasn't a house, Jones could see now, but a long L-shaped bungalow.

He ran towards the garage, which shielded him from the bungalow, and went inside.

The sight of the car stopped him short. He knew now that he was on the right track.

The car was the same model as the one he had seen outside C.P.'s flat. The same as the one into which he had seen Dingle being dragged . . .

He froze at the sound of footsteps on the path outside. Then he saw the ladder leading to the loft. When the man came into the garage, Jones was

lying down, peering through a crack in the rough
floorboards.

The man whistled softly under his breath as he
worked, changing the number plates on the car. Then
he cursed under his breath and spent some time search-
ing through tin boxes on the shelves which lined the
garage. Eventually he found what he wanted and resumed his work.

More footsteps sounded and someone else entered the
garage but stopped outside Jones's range of vision.

"You've been a hell of a long time, Turner. What's
keeping you?"

Jones stiffened as he recognised the voice. Dawes.

"Thread stripped on the bleedin' bolt. Took me ages
to find another one the right size. I've finished now
though."

"Good. I wanted to be in London by one. Doubt
if I'll make it before half-past now."

Dawes moved into sight and climbed into the driving
seat.

"Our friend Dingle is awake now. You'd better go
across and help Gunney and Chance to keep an eye on
him until I get back."

When the car and Turner had left, Jones sat with his
legs dangling through the loft entrance and considered
the situation.

Dingle was here, but guarded by three men. Three
against one—and an injured one at that—were not

favourable odds. On the credit side, there seemed to
be time to spare; at least until Dawes got back from
London.

Jones clambered down into the garage and retraced
his steps to the shrubbery behind the hangar. He re-
climbed the fence, walked back to the Lotus and drove
into New Romney to find a telephone.

" Is that you Willie?"

" Yes. Where are you Glyn?"

" New Romney."

" Ah! I see. Any luck."

" Yes. Jim's here. I want you to come down straight
away to give me a hand."

" I can't. I'm supposed to be looking for . . ."

" You've got some of your section working on that,
haven't you?"

" Yes, but . . ."

" Leave it to them then. I need you here."

" But the Director . . ."

" Tell him I said so. He's given me a free hand. Anyway, I don't think the girl's so important at the moment."

Williams sighed. " Okay, if you say so. I'll tell him.
Where shall I meet you?"

" At the railway museum in the miniature railway
station. Know it?"

" Yes, I'll leave as soon as I've seen the Director."

" Good . . . don't ring off. I want you to do something else first. Get on to SB and tell them we want Dawes's car followed. It's heading towards London now."

He gave Williams a description of the car and its registration number.

"Tell them we want to know exactly where he goes and who he meets; but we don't want him or any of his contacts to be approached or alerted in any way. SB will probably want quite a few men on the job to do it properly, so get a Priority One on it. The Director will authorise it for you."

"Righto Glyn. Will do."

"Oh! One more thing. We're going to need some equipment down here, so you'll have to draw it out of the stores and bring it down with you."

He told Williams exactly what to fetch.

*   *   *

Marjorie Brett sped past four cars and then squeezed in behind a heavy lorry just in time to avoid an on-coming petrol tanker.

"Slow down a bit," said Finn. "You might be suitably dressed, but I don't want it to be my funeral you're going to."

Mrs. Brett was wearing black: leather trousers, jacket and peaked cap.

She gave a tight smile and spun the wheel expertly,

pulling the Ford Zephyr out to overtake the lorry.

" Anyway," Finn went on, " there's no great hurry."

" I hope you're right," said Harry Brett. He was sitting between his wife and Finn on the wide front bench seat. " I hope Dawes is still at his house. How can you be so sure?"

" I'll tell you," answered Finn, who was obviously in a good humour. " It was quite easy in the end. I simply rang up his secretary and asked to speak to him. She said he wasn't in the office. He'd called in briefly earlier this afternoon, but he wouldn't be back today. So I asked if she knew where I could get in touch with him, and she said no, she didn't. Could she take a message?"

" Well, that doesn't mean he'll be at home," said Harry Brett.

" So I then said I was a close friend of Dawes and I had some highly important news for him. Then I asked, casually, if she thought I'd be able to reach him at his place in New Romney. She talked then. She said he was flying to Athens tonight—but he wasn't taking off from Heathrow until midnight."

" Heathrow? But that's . . ."

" But she happened to know his plane was still down in Kent this afternoon. He would be flying up from Kent this evening to evening to Heathrow to refuel and check through Customs and Immigration, or whatever it is they do, before leaving for Athens."

Finn beamed. " So there you are. He won't plan to

leave Kent before eight at the earliest; and it'll probably be much later."

He chuckled and added: " My own arrangements should tie in very nicely. Friend Dawes is in for a big surprise."

" I hope you're right," said Harry Brett for the second time. " And I hope we can find his house in the dark."

" Oh, stop worrying and enjoy the drive," said his wife, cutting in front of an indignant mini to avoid a head-on collision with a bus.

C.P., sitting in the back, shuddered and tightened his grip on Susan's hand.

He leaned over and whispered in her ear. " Sue, how did you come to be a . . . to get mixed up in this business? Did they approach you when you went to Russia after your parents were . . . after the accident?"

She turned to face him.

" For heaven's sake! Haven't you realised yet, I'm not Susan Pike. When the real Susan Pike came to Russia one of my superiors noticed how alike we were. From then on it was simple. She was questioned closely about her life, her job, her habits . . . and then I came back in her place. Luckily her parents hadn't lived long in Taunton, so they didn't have many close friends there. But just to be on the safe side I moved to London and took the job with the BBC."

" But what happened to . . . to the girl?"

" Oh, she's being taken care of," she answered

vaguely. "So if you're coming to Russia with me, you'd better get used to calling me Svetlana.

"My name is Svetlana Kemerovo."

* * *

"Where the hell are we going now?" asked Ritchie.

"Search me," repied Gruber.

"Well, wherever it is, we're well-equipped for whatever it is we're supposed to do," said Ritchie, screwing round to look into the back of the van. "That's what I like about our organisations. We're always working in the dark."

"And I'm driving in the dark," said Gruber. "If you don't stop yapping and let me concentrate, we won't be working any place any time."

The battered-looking old van rushed on through the night. Despite its appearance, it could match almost anything on the road for speed.

CHAPTER THIRTEEN

" CAN I have a cigarette?" asked Dingle.

Gunney looked up from his cards.

" Give him one, Turner."

Turner stood up and threw his cards on to the table.

" Count me out anyway," he said, pulling a packet of cigarettes from his pocket and walking to the bed where Dingle was still tied.

" I'd rather have one of my own," said the SS(O)S agent.

He looked at his suit hanging behind the door. They'd stripped him to his underwear while he was still unconscious last night, before tying him to the bed.

" Too bad," said Turner, unfastening Dingle's left wrist and handing him a cigarette. " It's this or nothing. Yours might be bugged for all we know." He flicked on his lighter.

Dingle inhaled the tobacco smoke deeply. He could jab the lighted end of the ciragette into Turner's face, he thought. But what good would it do? His right arm and his legs were still bound—and there would still be two other men to deal with.

He looked at his suit again. If only he could get at the pocket . . .

He shivered.

" Can't I have my jacket on? I'm bloody cold."

" No you can't," said Gunney.

" We've heard about clothes with gadgets sewn into them," added Chance.

" You've been reading too many spy stories," said Dingle.

" Get a blanket and throw it over him if he's cold," Gunney told Turner. " I'll see you," he added to Chance.

Dingle looked at his watch and felt a surge of frustration. Six o'clock already. It had been dark for a hour and the heavy curtains were drawn. Dawes would be back soon—and so far there hadn't been the slightest opportunity to escape.

He looked again at his jacket.

*   *   *

Jones and Williams sat at opposite sides of the loft opening, their legs hanging down into the garage.

" It's six o'clock and dark enough," said Williams. " I don't see why we shouldn't go into the house now. We could take them by surprise and get Jim out in no time."

" I know, Willie," answered Jones. " But just think it out. It isn't only Jim we want; we've got to get the films as well. The chances are that Dawes has them—he wouldn't leave important items like that with those three apes—and Dawes isn't here yet. We don't want him to be alerted so that he can escape with the films."

" If we went in now, we'd reduce the opposition for when Dawes does arrive," argued Williams.

" I'll grant you that. But he might get back just as we're dealing with his three mates—and that could make it awkward. Apart from that, we don't know how they're operating. Dawes might be in regular telephone contact with the house to make sure everything's all right at this end. If he smelt a rat he wouldn't be back. We can't risk losing those films, boyo."

*   *   *

Dawes was supremely confident. He swung off the A20 at Ashford to take the B road through Ham Street and Ivychurch to New Romney.

" We'll save a few minutes this way, Colonel," he said. " It's ten to six already."

" Yes. The sooner I renew my acquaintanceship with Mr. Dingle the better I shall be pleased. I am most anxious to learn how he came to know about Mr. Croome-Pugglesley's efforts on our behalf."

116

Colonel Fu Chang-sui's voice was light and rather high-pitched; his English precise and accentless.

"I haven't liked using you so openly," he went on. "Your undercover work is invaluable to us and it seems foolish to expose you to risk. But in a matter as important as the DNA File I had no choice. I hope that you haven't been . . . what do you call it? . . . blown by Mr. Croome-Pugglesley."

"I don't see how he could blow me. He only met me once, and I didn't tell him my name. If you think he might have contacted the authorities, forget it. He's too scared for his own neck to do that."

"It would be quite out of character, I agree," the Colonel conceded. "But there still remains the fact that Dingle knew exactly when and where the wretched man was going to leave the films for us."

"I think you'll find the answer is that SS(O)S have been watching C.P. ever since the Roger Coyle business," said Dawes.

"I do so hope you're right." The Colonel sighed. "However, we shall soon find out."

* * *

Marjorie Brett pulled off the road on to the grass verge and stopped.

"That must have been the place back there."

"Yes." Finn looked at his watch. "Six o'clock. Let's

go and take a look. It seems quiet enough at the moment
—and I'm sure we weren't followed."

"Why should we be followed," asked Harry Brett
in sudden alarm. "Who would know about us?"

"We weren't followed," said Susan. "I've been check-
ing on that."

"Of course we weren't," said Finn. "But it pays to
play safe Harry. Remember that. Now Marjorie and
I will go and carry out a reconnaissance. The rest of
you wait here."

* * *

"Shall I stop here?" asked Gruber.

"Yes, you'd better," said Ritchie. "There was a lay-
by a few yards back. Reverse into it."

The NSA man backed the van into the lay-by,
switched off the engine and dowsed the lights.

"Now what?" he asked.

His companion from the FBI didn't answer immediately. He appeared to be listening intently. Then he
said :

"We'll wait a couple of minutes, then I'll go and
have a look-see."

CHAPTER FOURTEEN

LIGHT FLOODED the garage, hit the ceiling and over-
flowed into the loft, exposing the rafters.

Jones and Williams, lying flat and peering down
through the cracks between the floorboards, felt exposed.
Then the car's headlamps went out, leaving them momentarily blinded. A door slammed.

"Wait a minute, Colonel. I'll switch the light on so
you can see your way."

Jones recognised Dawes's voice. Then, in the harsh
glare of the naked bulb, he saw Fu Chang-sui climb
out of the car.

"I won't stay long, Colonel. I'll take you to Dingle
and get Turner to fix some food for you, then I'll leave
for Heathrow. I'd like to get there as soon as possible
because, when I've refuelled, I've arranged for the
mechanics to check the aircraft. We don't want anything
to go wrong."

"Indeed we don't. You'll be back here to pick us up
soon after midnight?"

" That's right."

The two men were at the garage door now, and Dawes switched out the light.

" Good. Now take me to Dingle. I can't wait to see him again. I'm sure he'll be . . ."

The voices faded into the darkness outside.

" Well, what do you make of that?" whispered Williams.

" A Chink," replied Jones softly. " We thought they were behind all this, but this is the first proof we've had. He must be the boss man."

" Did you recognise him?"

" No. They all look the same to me anyway. Did you?"

" No. But he seems to know Jim. What now? Are we going in to bust up the party?"

Jones considered the question.

" Not yet. There are five of them and only two of us. They might win."

" For Pete's sake Glyn! We can't keep putting it off. We'd at least have the element of surprise on our side." He paused and then added: " Or shall I slip off and phone for reinforcements?"

" No, don't do that. Something might happen while you were away—and then it would be five against one. I think we'd better play it safe. Don't forget, the films are the main objective. We've either got to get them back; or destroy them."

" So?"

" So if we go into the house we'll be in trouble straight away. We don't know the layout of the place. We don't even know which room Jim is in. And we don't know which of them has the films."

" I should think the Chinese has them, if he's the boss."

" Possibly. Although they might be hidden somewhere in the house until they're ready to leave."

Williams sighed. " All right, so what's your latest brilliant idea in strategy?"

" You heard what Dawes said. He's flying to Heathrow, then he's coming back just after midnight to pick up the Chinese chap. It's a racing certainty that when the Colonel comes out to board the plane, either he or Dawes will be carrying the films."

" I see," said Williams slowly. " You mean we take them when they come outside?"

" That's it. That way everything will be on our side. We can take them by surprise when they step out of the lighted house into the dark. If they try to make a fight of it we can pick them off easily. They won't have a clue where we are. There's plenty of cover in the garden; bushes all over the place. They'll probably think they're surrounded by a bloody army."

Williams was convinced.

" Okay. We'll give it a try."

" That's the spirit boyo. Now shine a light and let's

check over the equipment you brought with you. We've
got plenty of time."

*　　*　　*

The jet raced down the runway and then left the
ground at a steep angle. As soon as it had taken off, the
runway lights were dowsed.

Finn, standing in the bushes behind the hangar, turned
to his companions.

"There he goes. Those lights were useful. They
should have given you a good idea of the line of the
runway. You know where to go now?"

The others nodded.

"Julian, Susan and I will be stationed in a row along
the bottom of the runway while you and Marjorie stay
at this end," said Harry Brett.

"Correct. And then?"

"Then we three will join you near the plane as soon
as it lands while Marjorie moves over to guard the main
gate and make sure we're not interrupted."

"Good. Now we've quite a wait on our hands, so
we might as well sit in the car. We'll be warmer and
more comfortable there."

*　　*　　*

"Who the hell do you suppose was in that plane?"
asked Ritchie.

" Search me boy," said Gruber.

" I wish I knew what was going on around here," the FBI agent said.

" Me too. Although I've a feeling we'll be finding out before long. One thing I'm certain about," the man from NSA went on, " we were right to worry about the safety of the DNA File."

" Yeah. These goddamn Limeys . . ." Ritchie placed a wad of gum in his mouth and carefully put the wrapping back in his pocket . . . " their Intelligence services are about as secure as a suspender from my fat Aunt Jemima's cast off corsets."

" You've said it, Son. I reckon their inefficiency is matched only by those blockheads in the pickle factory," agreed Gruber, who detested his CIA rivals. " So what's our next step?"

" I'll keep watch here," said Jason Ritchie. " You take a look at our friends. If they seem settled for a bit, come back here."

" Right."

" And bring the gear with you out of the van. I think we're going to need it."

CHAPTER FIFTEEN

"My dear Mr. Dingle, how nice to meet you again."

"Colonel Fu. I'm sorry I can't shake hands with you. I'm a bit tied up at the moment."

"Ah! The English sense of humour. I like that." He smiled as he advanced towards the bed. "So . . . you won the last battle, but I win the war. Isn't that an old English proverb?"

"I don't know about it being old English . . . we probably pinched it from Confucius. But the war isn't over yet, Colonel."

"It is for you, my friend. It is for you. I'm taking you back with me to China. We have some unfinished business there. Remember?"

Dingle remembered. He had been arrested in Canton by Fu's men—and had escaped while being transported to Peking.

"I almost lost my job over that affair," Fu went on. "But we shall discuss the . . . ah . . . details of your escape more fully when we are back in China."

Dingle looked at the smooth, smiling, gentle face of the Chinaman; and then beyond, into the dark depths of expressionless eyes which no smile could reach. There was no colour contrast between pupils and irises, and the eyeballs were a muddy brown. Evil eyes.

" You'll have to get me there first."

The British agent smiled back confidently, and Fu seemed to read his thoughts.

" It will be easy, I can assure you, Mr. Dingle. And if you imagine your friend Jones is going to rescue you, forget it. He was shot last night. If it makes you feel any better, he was shot while trying to . . . ah . . . deny us the pleasure of your company."

Dingle felt sick.

" And as I said," Fu continued, enjoying the moment, " it will be easy to get you out of the country in my colleague's plane. It's the way I came in."

" You must rate this business as highly important to risk coming here yourself, Colonel."

" Risk? There is no risk Mr. Dingle. Your country is so hospitable. Black, brown, yellow . . . what difference does it make. One more Chinese face here isn't going to excite any comment or curiosity. Of course, I was careful not to go near our legation. I didn't want to be recognised by the Special Branch people who watch the place.

" And naturally we regard this DNA breakthrough

as important. So do you and the Americans. So will the Russians, if they know about it."

The black eyes began to gleam fanatically as the Chinese continued to speak rapidly.

" The Americans have discovered it, but they will be reluctant to take it to its logical conclusion. They are too frightened of offending world opinion. But we shall develop it until . . ." He paused and then added quietly. " Tell me, Mr. Dingle, don't you think it fitting that the most ancient civilisation on earth should be the one to produce a master race?"

The final words came out in a malicious hiss, filling Dingle with revulsion. He knew now that, at all costs, he must prevent this man from taking the secrets of the DNA File to China. And he had one hope.

Once more Fu seemed to read the SS(O)S man's thoughts. He smiled, in control of himself again.

" Perhaps I should tell you, Mr. Dingle, that I know you substituted fake films for the ones Mr. Croome-Pugglesley left in his biscuit barrel. My colleague, Mr. Dawes, found the originals in your pocket. I now have them." He held them up briefly before slipping them back into his overcoat pocket.

The hope died, but a new resolve was born in Dingle's mind. He would destroy the films—and himself with them.

" And don't imagine you will be able to sabotage the plane during the flight to Albania. You will be drugged."

The Chinese colonel's mind-reading ability was uncanny.

For the first time, Dingle began to fear the man.

CHAPTER SIXTEEN

FIFTEEN MINUTES to midnight. Fully dressed now, but
still securely bound, Dingle tensed at the faint sound
which was growing steadily louder. He saw that the
others had noticed it, too.

Colonel Fu Chang-sui looked at his watch.

"He's early."

"We'd better put the runway lights on, sir," said
Gunney.

The plane was overhead now, low, its engines throttled
back.

Fu nodded. "You and Mr. Chance can go and meet
Mr. Dawes, but Mr. Turner must stay here with me
and keep an eye on our friend."

He turned to Dingle as the two men left the
room.

"Not that you're likely to give us any trouble, eh?"
An earlier tension had left the Chinese officer now that
the aircraft had arrived. He seemed almost jovial. "You
might as well relax Mr. Dingle and resign yourself to

the inevitable. In a few hours you will be in Albania. So stop worrying and enjoy the flight."

The SS(O)S agent couldn't deny that he was worried. But he had not yet begun to despair; he was still alert, waiting for the slightest chance to thwart the Chinese plan. " I can hardly expect to enjoy the flight if I'm drugged," he said.

" Ah! Perhaps I should explain," the colonel said. " You will not be given the drug until just before we land at Rome to refuel.

" We shall not disembark there, so no officials are likely to bother us. But if anyone does board the plane, we have papers to prove that we are technical experts en route to Athens to help Mr. Dawes clinch his sales deal. Mr. Dawes will explain that you have taken a strong sleeping draught because you always feel unwell in an aeroplane."

" Which would be true," said Dingle, who hated flying. He had once been the sole survivor of a Service aircraft crash.

" I should add," Fu went on, " that apart from the time we are actually on the ground at Rome, your hands and feet will be tied. You will be carried from this room to the . . ." he broke off abruptly, listening. " Ah! They're coming."

He looked at the door, smiling a welcome for Dawes.

* * *

Jones and Williams stood outside the garage listening to the aircraft circling above.

" Must be Dawes," said the Welshman. " A bit earlier than he thought he'd be."

" Perhaps he . . . hullo! The runway lights have been switched on."

" Quickly, boyo. Let's get behind the hangar," Jones whispered urgently, starting to run.

They reached the deep shadow at the rear of the hangar and peered round the corner, just in time to see the nose of the aircraft coming straight towards them, leaving the runway at an angle.

" Christ, man! He's going to park here, on the apron," said Williams breathlessly.

" The bushes. Over there," said Jones, leading the way to the shrubbery at the edge of the apron.

They reached cover and sank down on their haunches as the plane taxied round and halted in the shadows behind the hangar, where they had been a few seconds earlier. Gradually, the whine of the engines died away.

" For Christ's sake, be quiet," hissed Jones. " You're panting like a bloody steam engine."

" It's all right for you," retorted Williams, aggrieved. " I'm carrying all the damn gear. Remember?"

" Well, I'm supposed to be convalescent, boyo. My neck's giving me . . . ssh! Here comes the welcome home committee."

*   *   *

Gunney and Chance ran along the side of the hangar.

" Why the hell has he parked right up here?" asked Chance.

" Dunno . . . probably wants to be out of the lights in case any other planes up top get curious. It's an unscheduled stop, don't forget."

The cabin door was open, the steps were folded down and the interior lights were out by the time they reached the aircraft. At the foot of the steps they paused uncertainly.

" Here!" exclaimed Gunney. " This . . ."

Two men appeared suddenly at the top of the steps.

" Just be quiet and stand exactly where you are," said the first slowly, in heavily accented English.

" Who the hell are . . .?"

" Quiet, I said, and don't move."

Gunney and Chance kept very quiet; and they stayed very still.

It was dark—but not too dark for them to see that the revolvers pointing at them were big enough to silence them forever and make movement impossible.

Footsteps sounded behind them. Someone must have been waiting inside the hangar, Chance thought. More footsteps, running this time. From the corner of his eye he glimpsed three silhouettes, outlined by the landing lights, coming from direction of the runway.

The footsteps behind him stopped; a voice called out something in a language Chance didn't understand. The man on the steps laughed and answered in the same foreign tongue.

Then the three others had joined them, out of breath after their run. In the darkness Gunney and Chance could just make out that one of them was a girl.

The man behind them spoke again, in English this time.

" You can turn around now, my friends," said Finn.

They turned, slowly, and saw that he had a gun, too. So did the girl and one of her two companions. The two men from the plane came down the steps and closed in behind them.

Finn was smiling.

" And now," he said gently, " as they say in the best science fiction novels—take us to your leader."

*　　*　　*

" Who the hell are that lot?" asked Williams as Chance, Gunney and their captors walked towards the bungalow and vanished from sight.

" I don't know—but they were speaking Russian, boyo."

" That's all we need. Now we're hopelessly outnumbered. I told you we should have attacked the house earlier. We might have had a chance then."

"Don't start nagging me, Willie bach. I'm trying to bloody think. Let's take a look at this plane."

They broke cover and walked softly across the apron.

"It's Russian all right, Willie. Look. No wonder the pilot's parked it in the shadows."

In the darkness they could just make out the Russian markings.

"Yes, I can see that. But what are we going to do?"

"For a start you can hop aboard and make sure there's nobody else inside. Then we'll go over to the house and see what's going on there."

Glyn Jones's brain was working furiously, and he had the germ of an idea. He looked at his watch.

"Dawes should be back any minute—if he's coming. I think we might still be able to pull something out of the fire."

CHAPTER SEVENTEEN

Fu CHANG-SUI'S welcoming smile froze, then faded as Gunney and Chance were propelled into the room.

"On your feet, Colonel," snapped Finn. He gestured towards Turner. "And you. Quickly."

Turner, sickly pale, jumped to obey. Fu rose more slowly. They stood quite still—looking into the business ends of five revolvers.

"Turn round, line up over there and lean forward with your hands flat against the wall. All of you! No, feet further out than that . . . that's better."

Finn moved behind them and ran his hands over them expertly. Quickly, he relieved Turner and Gunney of their automatics and Chance of his cosh. He found nothing on Fu.

"I don't carry weapons," said the colonel.

Finn grunted and jerked him upright by the back of his collar.

"Over to the table and empty your pockets," he ordered.

As Fu crossed the room, Dingle, still lying tied to the bed, raised his head and grinned.

"Unexpected company, eh Colonel Fu." He craned his neck to look at Croome-Pugglesley. "Nice to see you C.P. old boy. Good of you to drop in."

C.P. didn't reply. He knew that if he opened his mouth to speak he would be sick. He had lived with fear for days; but now it was spreading inside him like an incurable cancer. All he wanted to do was run . . . anywhere.

Nervously, he eyed the guns that had been dumped on the table. He hoped Fu would not make a grab for one. Finn's men would retaliate if Fu and his party decided to resist. Lead would fly; and if he got in the way of a stray bullet . . . Beads of cold sweat formed on his brow. He jerked at the sound of his name.

"So, Mr. Croome-Pugglesley, you have been playing a double game," said Fu. "And your friends have come to rescue you in the nick of time, Mr. Dingle."

Finn laughed.

"Dingle is no friend of ours. You're welcome to do what you like with him—after we've gone."

"Then who are you?" asked Fu slowly.

"I and my colleagues are agents of the KGB. Mr. Croome-Pugglesley has decided to join us. And these two gentlemen are Russian pilots who have been recruited for the occasion."

"And what do you want? The films that Mr. Croome-Pugglesley obtained for me?"

"How did you guess? Now stop wasting time and hand them over."

Fu shook his head slowly.

"I haven't got them."

Finn's voice hardened.

"I can shoot you first and search you afterwards. It's up to you. Now, empty your pockets."

Fu shrugged and obeyed. There were no films among the items that littered the table after he had finished.

"Now pull out the linings of your pockets so I can see them."

The linings were clean.

Finn once more ran his hands over Fu's clothing. He patted the colonel's back pocket.

"What's this?"

"Ah! I forgot that pocket." There was a faint smile on the Chinaman's lips. "It's a hip flask."

Finn pulled it out roughly. He unscrewed the can and let it drop so that it hung by the short silver chain attached to the side of the flask.

"A conveniently wide neck," he said, sniffing the liquid inside.

"It's very good brandy," said Fu. "Try some."

Calmly, Finn poured the drink over the carpet. Then he probed the inside of the flask with a thin pen.

Fu sighed.

136

"You're wasting your time. The films aren't in there."

"Then where are they?"

Finn was angry now.

"In the plane. Dawes has them. He'll be here soon, as you probably know, since you seem to be so well informed."

Finn took a pace forward. "Now look here . . ."

"It's true," Dingle interrupted him.

The British agent's thoughts were racing. He knew the Chinese colonel had the films. They were in the pocket of his overcoat which was hanging inside the wardrobe. Any delay might be turned to advantage, he thought. When Dawes arrived, Fu and his gang might make a fight for it. Then anything could happen.

"How do you know?" Finn's voice was harsh.

"I saw Fu give them to Dawes before he took off."

Finn hesitated. Then he looked at his watch and shrugged.

"Very well. We'll wait. He's due any minute now."

Fu turned his black eyes on Dingle and gave a slight smile. Dingle knew that, once again, the colonel had read his thoughts.

"Tell me Mr. er . . .?"

"Finn."

"Mr. Finn. How did you know about my mission?" Fu asked. "And how did you know where to find me?"

" It was easy. We've been keeping a close watch on
Mr. Croome-Pugglesley, Julian, ever since your scheme
with Coyle went wrong. Svet . . . er Susan here was
assigned to the task."

Casually, Fu began to pick up his belongings and put
them back into his pockets.

" And how did you find me here?"

" That, too, was easy. After we had persuaded Julian
to join us, he identified Dawes for us, and all we had
to do was . . ."

" But I was assured that Mr. Croome-Pugglesley
didn't know Dawes' name—and they only met once."

" That's true. Dingle told Julian about Dawes."

" Ah! so! SS(O)S know about him? Dawes is . . . er
. . . blown?" Again Fu turned his expressionless eyes on
Dingle.

" Blown wide open, my old china," said Dingle cheerfully.

" One more thing." said Fu. " How were you able to
get a Russian aircraft here so quickly and conveniently?"

" A Soviet team is in this country at the moment taking
part in the aerobatic championships. This plane is one
of the team's supply aircraft. I was able to arrange for
it to leave Heathrow for Russia tonight to pick up some
spare parts.

" I and my colleagues were already down here,
stationed on the landing strip with signalling lamps to

guide it in. As it happened it didn't matter; someone kindly switched on the runway lights and . . ."

Finn broke off suddenly, listening intently. Then he added : " If I'm not mistaken, your Mr. Dawes has arrived."

He turned to the two pilots and spoke rapidly to them in Russian.

The men nodded and left the room.

" And you, Colonel," Finn went on, " can rejoin your friends against the wall."

CHAPTER EIGHTEEN

WILLIAMS AND Glyn Jones had completed a circuit of
the bungalow. They had seen a sliver of light through
the heavy curtains of one window, and had heard the
murmur of voices coming from inside the room. Now
they stood near the path leading to the back door, in
the shadow of a tree. The runway lamps were still burning—but their light didn't reach this far.

" Shall we go in?" whispered Williams. " They all
seem to be in one room. We might find Jim in one of the
other rooms."

" I doubt it. He's probably in with them, where they
can watch him. And Dawes isn't here yet, don't forget."

" We'll hear the plane when . . ."

" And so will the others. What do you think they'll do
then, boyo?"

Williams thought for a moment.

" Probably send a couple of men out to pick him
up."

" That's what I think. If we wait here, we can take

them as they come up the path. Then we can go and take care of Dawes ourselves."

" Reduce the opposition you mean, before we go in?"

" That's it, boyo. We can just walk in then and surprise 'em. Take a leaf out of the Russians' book; that's what they did to the Chinks. Have you got any rope in that box of tricks you're carrying, Willie?"

" Yes."

" Good. We'll need it to . . ." he stopped speaking abruptly and gripped Williams's arm. " Listen!"

" I hear it. Coming in low."

" Must be Dawes. Someone will be out in a minute. Get behind that bush on the other side of the path. When they walk past we'll take them from behind."

" Right." Williams nodded and moved away.

Only seconds later the back door opened, spilling a shaft of light on to the path. Two men came out and stood talking for a few moments, looking about them. Then the door was closed, shutting off the light.

Now Jones could see the men only as vague shapes, but they didn't come up the path. There was a porchway over the back door—and in the angle it formed with the bungalow wall was a large rainwater barrel. One of the men hid behind it. The other crouched behind the dustbin on the other side of the porch.

Damn! Jones got down on his stomach and crawled across the path to Williams.

" The bastards aren't coming. They're hiding one on

each side of the porch. They aim to get Dawes as he goes through the door."

"What now?"

"We'll have to deal with Dawes first." The noise from the aircraft was deafening now. "Come on! I think he's touched down."

*   *   *

Dawes noticed nothing amiss. He couldn't see the Russian plane parked in the shadows behind the hangar.

He landed rather heavily and then braked hard, using up less than half of the runway to bring the jet to a stop a hundred and fifty yards in front of the hangar.

He taxied round and parked, as close to the bungalow as he could, ready for take-off. It would be a short take-off, he thought. But there was no sense in wasting time. The sooner they were off the ground again, the better.

He moved out of the cockpit, opened the cabin door, and unfolded the steps. As he came down he saw the two figures coming round the tail to meet him.

"That you Gunney?"

"'Fraid not," answered Jones. "Just put your hands up, very high, and keep them there."

Dawes saw the gunmetal glinting in the light from the cabin doorway. He raised his hands.

"Right. Check the plane Willie. Quick as you can."

Williams disappeared inside the aircraft. A few moments later he was back.

"All okay. There's nobody else aboard," he reported.

Jones pushed Dawes in the back.

"Now move," he ordered. "To the hangar, at the double."

The three of them began to trot, Williams still carrying his heavy bag.

"Who the hell are you?" asked Dawes as they entered the hangar.

"Shut up! Willie, shine a light and get the rope."

Williams flicked on his torch, placed it on the floor so that it pointed at Dawes, and fished in his bag for the rope.

"Lie on your belly, hands behind your back," snapped Jones. "Come on! Move!"

Williams tied the pilot's hands and feet, then gagged him. It was all done very quickly and expertly.

"Come on Willie bach, we mustn't keep the reception committee waiting. You can leave your bag here. Pick up your torch. Shine it in front of you as you go up the path to keep their attention on you. They'll think you're Dawes. But give me time to approach the house from the garage side.

"When you get to the back door, the two Ruskies will come up behind you. But then I'll be behind them and have the drop on them. Got it?"

Williams nodded.

"Yes. But why me? Why don't you walk up the path and let me take them from the rear?"

"Because they might be planning to hit Dawes on the head, or shoot him or something."

"Oh."

"Now get going."

Williams nodded again and began to walk. He stopped suddenly.

"Hey!"

But Jones had already gone.

"You cunning bloody Welsh rarebit," muttered Williams as he started to walk again.

* * *

Jones slipped silently around the back of the garage —then halted abruptly as something solid blocked his path. Something else, equally hard, jabbed him in the back.

"Drop your gun and put your hands on your head."

The Welshman went cold. His gun dropped from nerveless fingers. Damn! They'd left it too late. They'd taken too long in dealing with Dawes and the Russians had come to investigate.

A light flashed in his face.

"Well, I'll be . . . It's that goddamn Limey."

In the reflected glow of the torch, Jones recognised Ritchie. He spun around and saw Gruber.

" Thank God it's you," he said. " Come on! No time
to explain—but my mate's walking into trouble. Follow
me, but don't make any noise."

*   *   *

Williams had his hand on the door handle before the
Russians closed in on him, one on each side. He felt a
small circle of cold metal pressed against his neck.

" Be still with the arms high," said a thickly-accented
voice.

The torch was taken from his hand; his clothing was
patted until the automatic was located and removed
from his shoulder holster.

" And now be walking slow in front of we. Open door
now."

Williams was bathed in a cold sweat. He shivered as
he reached again for the door knob. Where the hell was
Jones?

" Drop your guns! You're surrounded," came the
Welshman's voice in perfect Russian.

Two revolvers clattered to the ground and the pilots
wheeled round in shocked surprise.

Williams turned, too.

" Right on cue Glyn," he said. " Hullo! Who are
they?" he added looking in astonishment at Gruber and
Ritchie.

" Friends," replied Jones tersely as he leaned forward

145

to push the door open. "Lead on MacTarovich," he added to the bigger of the two Russians.

Gruber picked up the discarded weapons and dropped them into his pockets as he followed the others into the bungalow.

The pilots halted at the door of the room in which Finn was waiting for them. At a nod from Jones, one of the Russians opened the door; then the two of them were pushed in, followed quickly by their captors.

"Drop your guns," shouted the Welshman. "The house is surrounded by police, so don't try to resist."

Harry Brett and Susan obeyed immediately—but Finn reacted instinctively. He spun around, dropped to one knee and squeezed the trigger twice.

The first bullet sang past Jones, waist high, and went out through the open door. The second went off at a tangent in C.P.'s direction when Finn's fingers were smashed by a shot from Ritchie.

It was an impressive display of marksmanship by the American, during which his jaws never ceased their rhythmical chewing action.

"Anyone else want to argue?" he inquired casually in the sudden hush which followed the shooting.

Nobody argued. And then the silence was broken by the sound of C.P.'s body thudding to the floor.

That second stray bullet from Finn had missed C.P.'s ear by a hair's breadth—and he had fainted.

Gunney, Chance and Turner, all deathly pale, were

146

still standing against the wall with Colonel Fu, who was smiling slightly. Jones ordered Finn and his party to sit on the floor in front of them.

Only then, with the Americans standing guard, did the Welshman look at Dingle.

" All right, Jim boyo."

" Fine. It's beginning to get a bit crowded in here though. It's time we left."

" You're bloody right. Cut those ropes Willy."

" I must say," Dingle added while Williams worked at his bonds, " you're doing very well for a man who is supposed to be dead. I was told you were shot last night."

" Oh I was boyo. Got up off my sick bed to get you out of this jam."

Dingle grinned. " Thanks. What have you done with Dawes, by the way?"

" He's all right. We've left him tied up in the hangar . . . Hurry up Willy!"

" Nearly done."

The rope fell free and Williams began to massage Dingle's legs to restore the circulation.

A moan came from Croome-Pugglesley as he struggled to sit up.

" Hello Seepy," said Jones. " You're not dead after all. There's lovely for you." He turned to Dingle. " Whose side is he on now? I'm getting a bit confused."

" At the last roll-call he was with the Russians," said Dingle.

" Tut tut Seepy. There's bad company you're keeping. You do chop and change don't you? You'd better come back to us."

Misery had temporarily swamped C.P.'s fear. He felt tired and ill. There was no hope for him now; he would rot in jail.

" Damn you," he muttered wretchedly. " It's all your fault that I'm in this mess."

But Jones didn't hear. He was watching Dingle, who was moving across the room to pick up one of the guns taken from the Russians.

Dingle grinned. " I'm okay now."

" I'm not," said Finn, who was sitting grimacing with pain, nursing his shattered hand. " I need medical attention."

" You'll get it," snapped Jones. " The prison doctor will have you as right as rain before you stand trial. In the meantime get your girl friend to wrap her scarf around it."

Susan snatched the silk square from her head and began to bind Finn's wound.

Dingle stood looking at the prisoners.

" We're going to need transport to cart this bunch off," he said. " One of us had better find the phone and order a couple of black marias."

" Right," agreed Jones. " But first of all, what about

the films? Have you still got them, or has one of these jokers pinched them?"

" I haven't got them, but I know where they . . ."

He didn't complete the sentence. Nobody was listening anyway. Everyone else in the room was staring at something in the doorway behind him.

Dingle turned—and looked into the eyes of a black Angel of Death.

CHAPTER NINETEEN

FEET BRACED apart, left shoulder hunched forward, her black leather jacket and trousers gleaming from the light drizzle that had began to fall outside, Marjorie Brett stood just inside the room.

The instrument of death which she cradled with a disconcerting professionalism was a Schmeisser MP40.

Dingle recognised it immediately and automatically catalogued it in his mind; sub-machine gun, 9mm., 28-round detachable magazine, folding metal stock, extended length 35 inches, loaded weight $10\frac{1}{2}$lb.

He looked carefully at the way she was holding it and guessed that, if she squeezed the trigger, it would pull to the right and slightly high; but only slightly. If she swung the gun in an arc, the stream of bullets would be low enough to scythe down every person standing in the room.

Finn and his group might escape. They were all squatting on the floor.

Dingle considered dropping flat. He could probably

get away with it—alone. But before he could get a
shot in that ugly black machine-pistol would be spurt-
ing death. He dismissed the idea. The risk to his friends
was too great.

All these thoughts flashed through his brain in the
instant before Marjorie Brett spoke.

" Drop your guns and remain exactly where you are."

Her tone brooked no argument. The words were
spoken quietly, yet they had a crispness which jolted her
listeners like an electric charge.

Ritchie, like Dingle, had weighed up the possibilities.
His gun thumped dully on to the carpet followed by
Dingle's, Gruber's and Williams's. Finally, Jones gave a
tiny shrug of resignation, opened his fingers and allowed
his revolver to fall.

The Schmeisser was a powerful persuader.

The tension in the room eased fractionally and, for
the first time, Mrs. Brett looked at her leader.

" I was guarding the main gate, like you said, when
I heard shooting. So I ran to the car and fetched this."
She made a tiny movement with the Schmeisser.

Finn's triumphant smile masked his pain.

" Well done Marjorie. I was relying on you—but
Jones said the house was surrounded."

" He's lying," she replied confidently. " I went right
round the place before I came in."

" Good. I'll join you."

Finn crawled across the floor, keeping as low as

possible, so that her arc of fire would not be interrupted. He collected Ritchie's gun on the way, holding it in his left hand, and stood up when he reached her side. Then he ordered the rest of his group to do the same, one at a time—while the SS(O)S men and the Americans were herded back against the wall with Fu's party.

Mrs. Brett's eyes flicked across the room.

" Where's Dawes?" she asked.

" In the hangar, according to Jones, tied up," answered Finn. He turned to the pilots and spoke in Russian. " Go to the hangar and bring back the man you will find there. Can I trust you to do the job properly this time?"

The pilots grunted in reply, and went out.

" Why fetch him?" asked Mrs. Brett.

" Because he has the films. At least, that slit-eyed PLA colonel says he has . . ." He broke off and added urgently : " Hey! Get back! Come round this way, behind me."

Croome-Pugglesley, hope and strength rekindled, was trying to reach Sue's side—and he had strayed into no-man's land. He stepped back quickly and made his way behind Finn and Mrs. Brett.

" What are you doing over there Seepy?" Jones called out. " You're on the wrong side man. Come over here with us."

Anger overruled the fear which still lurked inside C.P., the fear which he knew would not desert him until he was safely behind the protection of the Iron Curtain.

" Leave me alone, damn you Jones. You're responsible for my position. You've ruined my career, my life in this country. Now let me go and build a new future with Susan . . ." he put an arm around the girl's shoulder . . . " We're going to be married as soon as we get to Russia."

"Bloody 'ell man, don't do it. Stay here. Get the girl to stay with you. The Director will work something out for you. Remember . . ." Jones searched his memory, recalling C.P.'s predilection for Latin phrases . . . *" coelum non animum mutant, qui trans mare currunt—* people who cross the sea change their sky but not their— affections. You wouln't be happy in Russia."

" You forget Jones. If I remain here, there will be no sky for me; only the ceiling of a prison cell. How many years do you think I would get for spying against my own country?"

" Dammit Seepy, you're not a real spy; not by choice anyway, only by default. We know that. The Director will probably get the charge reduced. You wouldn't serve long . . ."

" Blandae mendacia linguae." C.P. cut him short. " The falsehoods of a smooth tongue. And, my God, Jones, you've got a smooth tongue; but you won't talk me into anything else."

" All right, that's enough you two," said Finn, who

had been listening to the exchange with amused interest. " Be quiet now. They're coming back."

He turned to face the door, covering it with his revolver, and signalled Brett and Susan to do the same. He didn't intend to be caught napping again. Marjorie Brett continued to menace the prisoners with the machine-pistol.

The door swung open and Dawes came in between the Russian pilots. His hands were still tied behind his back.

" Ah, Mr. Dawes. You have something for me, I hope."

Dawes blinked in the glare of the electric light.

" I don't understand."

" The films, man! Give them to me."

" He doesn't have them," Fu's smooth, precise voice came from the other side of the room.

Finn whirled around to face him.

" I'm afraid I must confess to an earlier deception," the Chinese colonel continued blandly. " Merely a ploy to gain time in the hope that when Mr. Dawes arrived he would sense that something was wrong and find a way to regain the initiative for us. But now," he shrugged and gave a curious half-smile, " I acknowledge defeat.

" I have the films. I engineered the whole plan to steal the secrets of the DNA File—of whose existence I believe you knew nothing—and now it seems I must hand them over to you. It is most unfair. Do you think perhaps Russia would be willing to share the information with China?"

"I'll mention it when I'm next in the Kremlin," said Finn sarcastically. "Now where are they?"

Fu shrugged again. "In the wardrobe, in my overcoat pocket. I'll get them for you." He began to move forward.

"No you don't," snapped Finn. "I'll get them."

He moved quickly across to the wardrobe and opened the door.

"This coat?"

"Yes. In the left hand pocket."

Finn found it awkward to work with his damaged hand. He pocketed his gun and, with his left hand, pulled out the coat, still on its hanger. He hooked it over the wardrobe door. Eagerly, he groped for the nearest pocket.

Fu's expressionless eyes watched him intently.

"No, not that one. I said the left hand pocket."

Finn pushed, suspicion darkening his face.

"You seem a little too anxious, Fu. Why? It is booby-trapped?"

"You're being absurd. I offered to get them for you myself."

Finn wasn't convinced.

"Julian! Come here. Put your hand in this pocket."

"No! I . . . I . . ."

The gun was back in Finn's hand. It was pointed at Croome-Pugglesley's chest.

"If you're coming with us, Julian, if you're going to marry Susan, you must work for us."

C.P. moved forward slowly on shaking legs. His eyes were wide with terror, sweat streamed down his pallid face, and his inside was turning to water. He stopped beside the coat.

Finn backed away.

"Now Julian."

There was utter silence in the room. All eyes were focused upon C.P.'s trembling fingers as, with terrifying care, they found the slit at the top of the pocket. The fingers disappeared inside; then the hand; then the wrist. The cloth of the coat moved as the fingers groped inside. The movement ceased.

"Anything there?" Finn's question was an explosion in the quietness.

C.P. closed his eyes and nodded dumbly. Then suddenly he withdrew his hand.

"Well?"

He unclenched his fist to reveal the tiny films nestling in his palm.

Seconds later, they were safely in Finn's pocket.

The KGB agent was in a hurry now.

"Right! We've got what we came for. Let's go."

He turned to the pilots and ordered them to get the aircraft engines started.

" Sue, Harry, Julian, you follow them and get aboard the plane quickly. But first, pick up all the guns that are lying around here and take them with you. Marjorie and I will stand guard until we hear the engines start."

" C.P. !" Jones called urgently. " Don't go with them."

" Go to hell."

" For God's sake man, stay here where you belong." There was desperation in the Welshman's voice. " We'll get something worked out."

C.P. paused in the doorway and looked back at Jones. Then, without speaking, he turned and went out.

" Come back !" yelled Jones. He took a pace forward.

" Stay still," snapped Finn.

Mrs. Brett increased the pressure of her finger on the machine-pistol's trigger. Jones saw the action and stepped back, with an anguished expression.

An engine coughed and whined into life; then another.

Finn and Mrs. Brett backed slowly into the hall. Then the door was slammed behind them.

*　　*　　*

Williams led the rush to the door. It was locked.

Gunney went in the opposite direction. He ripped the heavy curtains aside—and screamed in agony when, for the second time in just over twenty-four hours, Dingle clipped him hard on the jaw.

"Hold it!"

Nick Gruber, the American NSA man, had backed into a corner from where he could survey the whole room. He had a gun in each hand; the ones he had picked up and put in his pockets after they had disarmed the Russian pilots outside.

Colonel Fu broke the sudden silence.

"I'm afraid you will have to relinquish your weapons. If you refuse, we shall all die. I have a plastic grenade."

He moved where everyone could see him. In his left hand he was holding his whisky flask. The cap, still attached to the chain on the side of the flask, had been unscrewed. This he held in his right hand.

"Ingenious, isn't it? I have only to pull the chain, if you'll pardon the expression, to release the pin. A tube runs down from the neck and opens out at the bottom, like an inverted funnel. This section holds liquor and is designed to fool anyone who probes inside—as, indeed, it fooled that stupid Russian. The cavities are packed with a very powerful explosive.

"And I'll use it!" Fu's voice rose sharply, and for the first time Dingle saw expression light up those evil, black eyes. It was the light of madness.

"I've planned this mission, and I'd rather die than fail and return home in disgrace." He was shouting now. The short silver chain was held taut between his fists. "I'll give you three to lay those guns down on the floor. One . . . two . . ."

Gruber shot a look of despair at Ritchie, who nodded.
". . . Three."

Gruber stooped quickly and set the guns down.

"Now kick them into the middle of the room."

The NSA man obeyed.

"Pick them up Mr. Chance and use one to shoot off
the lock on the door."

Chance moved to the door. He fired twice, and the
door swung open.

"Good." Fu was in control of himself again. "Mr.
Dawes, go and start the plane."

"I will if someone unties these ropes," the pilot
replied. His hands were still bound behind his back.

"Mr. Gunney!"

Gunney stopped massaging his jaw and leapt to obey.
He began to work furiously on the knots.

Outside, the engines of the Russian plane were still
screaming.

"Why haven't they taken off yet?" asked Fu.

Dawes's experienced ear had been listening subcon-
sciously to the aircraft for some time.

"I think they're having trouble with one of the
engines, but it sounds sweeter now. They'll be off in a
minute."

The rope fell free.

"Shall I go now?"

Fu nodded. "I'll join you very shortly. Mr. Gunney,
Mr. Chance, Mr. Turner . . . thank you for your help.

Take the car from the garage. Leave it somewhere in London and disperse. You will be contacted when we need you again."

The SS(O)S men and the Americans were left alone with Fu.

" I'm sorry, Mr. Dingle, that I shall not be able to take you to Peking after all."

" Another time perhaps," said Dingle lightly.

Jason Ritchie spoke.

" Colonel, you said just now you would rather die than fail in your mission—but the Russians have the films."

Fu smiled. " Explain, Mr. Dingle."

" They've got the wrong ones," said Dingle. " They've taken the fakes I planted in Croome-Pugglesley's flat."

" Exactly." Fu moved across to the wardrobe.

He had to release the cap of the flask for a moment while he reached into the right hand pocket of the overcoat. But the distance between him and the five agents was too great for them to try to rush him.

The Chinaman held up the twin film cartridges for a moment before slipping them into his jacket and resuming his grip on the flask cap.

" These are the real ones."

They could hear the Rusian jet racing down the runway now. Added to its noise was the sound of more engines being run up. Dawes was ready for take-off.

" And now I must leave you," Fu continued.

He crossed with a cat-like tread to the doorway, his malignant black eyes never leaving them as he moved. When he reached the hallway he turned to run.

But before he turned, he ripped the chain from the flask, releasing the pin.

He tossed the grenade into the room.

CHAPTER TWENTY

DINGLE REACTED quickly, flinging himself flat—on top of the grenade. The others dived for cover behind the sparse furniture.

Nothing happened.

Then Dingle was rolling, snatching up the grenade; as he turned, he hurled it through the window.

The pane shattered noisily and the pieces broke into smaller fragments on the concrete outside.

There was a short, sudden silence; and then the rest of the glass in the window was punched inwards by the blast wave as the bomb exploded, showering the SS(O)S agent and cutting his face.

" Jim! You all right?"

" Yes. Must have been a fifteen-second fuse on that thing. Designed to give the user plenty of time to get away, I suppose."

" Fifteen seconds!" echoed Jones. " Bloody 'ell, boyo, is that all it was?"

" Long enough for me to age fifteen years, I guess,"

Ritchie butted in. He poked his head out from underneath the bed, still chewing steadily on his gum. " Is it safe to come out now?"

" You don't look any older," commented Gruber, emerging from behind the wardrobe. " But I've gone deaf." He wiggled his little fingers in his ears, shaking his head. " Whatever that little Chink kept in his liquour flask, it sure packed a punch."

Dingle was on his feet, running for the door.

" Come on!" he shouted urgently. " The bastard'll get away."

The others were close behind him when he reached the edge of the landing strip.

But there was nothing they could do, except stand and watch helplessly.

The earlier rain had cleared and a yellow moon rode high, outshining the stars, tarnishing their silvery glitter.

The five men could see the black outline of the Russian aircraft, climbing steeply, its nose probing ahead, reaching for the translucent sky.

Colonel Fu's plane was already near the end of the runway, just about to become airborne.

*   *   *

C.P. leaned back in his seat, breathing deeply, feeling the pressure in his back as the powerful jets lifted him from his native soil. He looked down at the dark landscape . . . at the country he might never see again.

Fear was receding now, with the white shore-line below; but a new anxiety was taking over. Was Jones right about Russia? Would he regret it later?

No, there must be no regrets; and with Sue to help him, there would be none.

He glanced at the girl sitting beside him, reached for her hand.

" We're safe, Sue," he whispered. " We're safe now."

She withdrew her hand.

" Sue . . .?"

" Svetlana. My name is Sveltana."

" I'm sorry. Svetlana. I'll try to remember."

He reached out to her again.

" Don't touch me!"

" But Sue . . . Svetlana! I'm . . ."

" Don't ever touch me again."

" I don't understand." He stared at her, bewildered. " We're going to be married as soon . . ."

" So! You don't understand! I loathe you, despise you, detest you. Is that clear enough for you. Until now, you were just another job to me. Now that job is finished. It's over. I don't have to pretend any more."

Anger rose inside him. Blind, unreasoning fury. He tried to get up. The seat belt restrained him; but it couldn't check the rage which blazed from his eyes and

then seemed to explode in his brain in a scorching red
ball . . .

*   *   *

The fiery red ball hung suspended in the sky for a
heartbeat; then, slowly, it disintegrated, like a spent
rocket on firework night. As the crippled Russian aircraft spiralled down, a second blast ripped through it.

The five agents, standing in the orange glow of the
landing lights, watched in awed fascination.

" Poor old Seepy," said Jones softly. " I tried to warn
him; tried to make him stay, but he wouldn't list . . ."

He broke off as yet another flash lit the heavens. For
an instant it silhouetted Dawes' aircraft; then that
machine too, seemed to separate into two parts as it
faltered and fell, down towards the sea.

Moments later the sounds of the explosions reached
the men on the ground.

Nick Gruber looked at his watch, a puzzled frown
wrinking his brow.

" That's darned funny. Those charges weren't due
to go off for another twenty minutes," he said.

Jones stared at him.

" Are you trying to tell us that you put bombs aboard
those planes?"

The American nodded.

" Sure we did. We had to do something to stop them

getting away with the DNA File. It was obvious that the lousy Limey security services couldn't prevent it."

"Bloody 'ell, boyo, I wish you'd told me," Jones said, peeved. "I could have saved some of our tax-payers' money."

"Whadya mean?" Jason Ritchie stopped chewing long enough to ask the question.

"Well, Willy and I stuck some bombs aboard too, see? In fact it's ours that went off. Limpet-type, attached to the outside of the fuselage, they were. Designed to explode as soon as the aircraft reached three thousand feet."

Dingle's face was pale beneath the bloodstains.

"While you were all going around sticking 'destination doom' labels on every plane in sight, did you realise that Fu Chin Chow planned to take me along as a passenger?"

Jones ignored the question. He was still glaring angrily at Gruber.

"And not so much of your 'Lousy Limey security'. You want to clean up your own backyard first.

"Red China has submarines that can fire missiles from under the sea now; the rockets have already been tested successfully. On top of that, China's made sudden leaps forward into space and atomic power.

"Why? Because their programme is being headed by Dr. Tsien Hsue-shen, a former top member of America's team of rocket scientists.

"So who's responsible for the big security muddle that allowed Tsien to return to China with his head stuffed with America's latest rocket secrets? Eh? Answer that, if you can.

"And as for this DNA business," Jones went on without pausing for breath, "you've been working at the wrong end. We can take care of security at this end —as you've just witnessed. But we told you before, the original leak . . . the leak that alerted the Chinese that C.P. was in charge of the file over here . . . must have come from your end."

"Okay, okay." Gruber held up his hands in mock surrender. "Touché. We've got some men working on it in America. As for the Dr. Tsien affair, it's probably the fault of those bums at the pickle factory . . . the CIA," he added bitterly.

"Anyway," said Jones. "How did you find your way down here?"

"Easy. We realised Croome-Pugglesley must be involved somewhere. Jason was following him while I checked up on the girl friend. We lost them for a while in the fog, but picked up the trail again at the dame's place and followed them to Ponder's End.

"Then that guy Finn turned up. From there on it was simple. We just bugged his car. They led us here."

"Very neat," said Jones grudgingly. "I'm sorry about Seepy, though. He was terrified out of his wits; didn't really know what he was doing."

"Well, he won't be frightened any more," commented Ritchie, interrupting his chewing once more. "He's dead."

"Death's no antidote to fear," said Jones. "It's a permanent bloody cure—for life."

EPILOGUE

POT-BELLIED clouds hung low over Whitehall. A strong wind whipped pebbles of rain against the conference room windows.

"You've seen the later editions of this morning's newspapers, gentlemen," said the Director. "A private company aircraft piloted by Mr. William Dawes was in collision over the Channel with a Russian aerobatics team supply plane. There were no survivors."

"That's the official story," said the D15 chief. "How long do you think it will be before the journalists smell a rat? They might spot the discrepancy in the times of take-off."

"We've put a security blackout on all information of that nature at Heathrow," the SB Commander broke in.

"And if all else fails, we'll slap a D-notice on the newspapers," the Co-ordinator added mildly. "Any bodies recovered yet, by the way?"

"Three," answered the Rear-Admiral (DSI). "In-

cluding the Chinese feller. Received a signal just before
I came here."

Gruber and Ritchie, who had been invited to sit in
on the Joint Intelligence Committee meeting as observers, leaned forward with interest.

"Found some films on him," the Naval officer went
on. "Bein' rushed up to London now."

"Excellent!" The Director gave ont of his rare smiles.
"All in all, a very good operation—thanks to your co-
operation C."

"Dangerous business, to mount an operation with top
secret material as bait, especially when it doesn't belong
to us," growled the head of D16.

"Oh, I think our American friends are satisfied that
the actual security of the DNA File was never seriously
threatened, aren't you, gentlemen?"

"Quite sure," lied Gruber easily. "We were never in
doubt. The whole affair has done us some good, too.
We received a message through our Embassy this morning, and the leak at the Washington end has been
plugged. The FBI unearthed quite an active cell of
Maoist workers."

"Excellent!" said the Director again. "We have
achieved similar results here. In fact that was the whole
object of the SS(O)S operation.

"We've been trying to smash the Chinese ring in this
country for some time.

"As you know, after Czechoslovakia, several local

Communist parties either split up or were disbanded altogether. But since then, several have re-formed, this time as Maoist groups.

" Colonel Fu Chang-sui was over here partly to organise the filching of the DNA File." The Director paused impressively. " But his prime motive was to co-ordinate these groups.

" He already had his group leaders, or officers, established in this country. Most of them were former anti-British Communist agitators from Singapore. They organised riots there when the British Army was containing the Communist threat from Indonesia."

" How the devil did they get in here then?" asked the General from the Ministry of Defence.

The Director frowned at the interruption.

" As students mainly, General. Don't ask me why they were allowed to stay. The ways of the Home Office are devious at times . . ."

" Get back to the point," muttered C.

The Director glared angrily at him.

" I will if people will stop interrupting. The point is, that when my agent, Jones, alerted us—and we in turn alerted SB—to follow Dawes yesterday . . . perhaps you'd like to take over from here Commander?"

The Special Branch chief beamed with pleasure.

" Dawes led us to a house in Camden Town where he met the Chinese colonel. There were other people there, and we didn't take any action; just observed, as the Director requested. Late last night, when the place was empty, we raided the house. Discreetly, of course.

" Everything was there; a complete list of all the Chinese ' officers' and all the Maoist sympathisers throughout the country—people like Gunney and the others who we've already heard about."

" Very nice work," admitted C grudgingly. " What action is being taken about them?"

" We've yet to decide. Either we can arrest the lot, or we can keep an eye on them. Alternatively we can infiltrate some of our own men into each group. But we can deal with that later," he added, glancing at the Americans.

" And of course," the Director resumed, " we had an unexpected bonus with the uncovering of Finn and his associates, thank to Mr. Ritchie and Mr. Gruber. The Commander's men found enough information at the Brett's house to smash another spy ring—Russian this time."

A murmur of approval sounded round the table and the Americans smiled in modest acknowledgement— until Ritchie felt the glare of the General's beady eye.

The FBI agent's smile vanished abruptly; he winced as he bit his cheek, and the rhythmical movement of his jaws ceased. He swallowed painfully.

The corners of the General's mouth twitched underneath his military moustache. Ritchie, glassy-eyed, tried to smile back.

He wondered how long that big goddamn wad of gum would take to travel down his throat.